MIDNIGHT MEETING

"Tell Tom Maus I'm back and I want to see him—I'm John Rourke."

A few moments later the door opened. Tom Maus, his good-natured, slightly gravelly sounding voice low, said, "You've been a busy man, Doctor Rourke—you and Major Tiemerovna have been very busy. Come in—"

"We have some friends with us—I wanted to tell you first."

"What kind of friends?"

"Two Soviet Special Forces officers and ten enlisted men—but they're on our side so to speak—"

Maus started to slam the door. Rourke stepped into it, pushing the door back. "Look—in a day, maybe six days at the most, nothing will be left. It's the end of the world, Maus—for real, the end of the world."

Rourke watched Maus's face in the grey-purple light.

"You're joking—and it's in poor—"

"I'm not joking," Rourke told him quietly.

"He is telling the truth," Rourke heard Natalia whisper beside him. "I wish to God he were not."

#9

THE SURVIVALIST

EARTH FIRE
BY JERRY AHERN

ZEBRA BOOKS
KENSINGTON PUBLISHING CORP.

ZEBRA BOOKS

are published by

Kensington Publishing Corp.
475 Park Avenue South
New York, N.Y. 10016

First printing: July 1984

Printed in the United States of America

For my wife Sharon (who is not Sarah), and for Jason Michael Ahern and Samantha Ann Ahern — all my love, always . . .

Chapter One

Reed jumped from the Jeep before it had fully stopped, shouting to his driver, "Get up the road to the high school and warn headquarters and tell 'em to pull out fast—use Emergency Plan Three—got that, Corporal?"

"Yes sir, but—"

"Just do it—move out—"

"What about you, Colonel—"

Reed started to run toward the grammar school building that had been converted to a field hospital—the wounded needed to be evacuated before the Soviet choppers struck. "I'll get transportation—now boogey, soldier!"

"Yes, sir!"

Reed hit the steps, taking them three at a time in a long strided run toward the front doors of the school building which more resembled an elaborate courthouse in some rich Eastern states county.

The guard just inside the door was clambering to his feet, getting his rifle up to present arms, Reed snarling, "Can it, soldier—get into the administrator's office—fast—tell him we're evacuating—we're using Emergency Plan Three—on the double, boy—"

"Yes, sir—"

Reed left the man gaping, punching through the inside doors and into the main corridor—the classrooms had been converted to laboratories and wards, the largest of the wards the lunchroom itself. But it was one of the smaller wards he ran toward—the only ward which housed the few female patients being treated. He sprinted along the corridor, shouting to one of the medical technicians, "We're evacuating—Soviet Air Cavalry unit five minutes away—maybe six—get some of these patients ready to travel, soldier!"

"But, Colonel Reed—"

"No buts—do it," and Reed sprinted on, reaching the end of the corridor, a nurse there, rather than white uniformed wearing clean but ragged fatigues that looked at least two sizes too big for her. "Nurse—start getting the patients ready," Reed snapped, dragging the woman toward him for an instant by the shoulders of her uniform. "We're movin' out fast—Russian choppers five or six minutes away!"

He didn't wait for an answer, taking the bend in the corridor left, running toward what had been one of the kindergarten rooms, skidding to a halt on the worn heels of his combat boots, twisting the doorknob and pushing inside.

There was space for three beds—but there was only one bed, a white-haired woman lying in it, sitting on the edge of the bed beside her a white-haired man. The man's face looked carved from stone—pain etched around the eyes, the jaw set. An IV tube ran between a half empty bottle and the woman's arm. Reed walked across the room to the bed. The man stood up. "Colonel Reed—"

Reed saluted, despite the tattered civilian clothes the man wore rather than a uniform. "Colonel Rubenstein—sir—there's a Soviet Air Cav Unit on the way—we don't have much time. Mrs. Rubenstein has to be moved."

Reed watched the older man's eyes flicker. "You're active duty—I'm just a retired Air Force officer. This is your show. But she can't be moved. You move the other ones, Colonel—my wife stays here. And I stay with her—"

"Sir, they're gonna—"

"I know what they're going to do, Colonel Reed—but she can't be moved. She's dying—she knows it. I know it. I'm not going to take the last few hours she might have left away from her—anymore than can't be helped anyway. If the Russians come, then maybe we'll both die together—"

8

Reed shook his head. "No — no — what about your son —"

"Paul would understand, Colonel —"

Reed shook his head again. "No, he wouldn't — if I were Paul Rubenstein, I wouldn't understand — you've got an obligation to live, sir. Your wife'd be the first one to tell you that — she'd —"

"That's enough Colonel — get out of here — let Paul's mother die in peace and maybe I can die with her —"

Reed balled his fists together along the outside seems of his fatigues. He opened his fists, turned around and found the doorknob, twisted it and stepped into the corridor. He wasn't seeing too well and he closed his eyes, leaning against the door for a moment as it closed. His own mother had died of cancer, and Paul Rubenstein's mother was doing the same.

"Shit," he snarled, hammering his fist against the wall. "Damnit it to hell!" He pushed away from the door. As he started running back along the bend in the corridor, he could hear the voice of the hospital administrator over the intercom — he was announcing the evacuation, that there was nothing to fear if order could be maintained. Nothing to fear — to Reed, since the Night of The War, there had been nothing but fear. Some little fear at times for his own safety, but when there was a job to do that required intelligence gathering against the enemy, there was no time for personal fear. But fear — that the War would never end, fear that the Russians could never be displaced from the power they had seized in North America, fear that the guy you shared a smoke with was someone you'd never see again. After the evacuation of the Florida peninsula before the mega-quakes which severed it from the continental U.S., he had come to know the Rubensteins like a second set of parents, suffered with them both when it had been learned Mrs. Rubenstein was dying of bone cancer and nothing could be done to save her. He had come, in the precious little time since the discovery of the rapidly progressing disease, to accept her death as inevitable, but not the death of her husband who had become, even more since the nature of Mrs. Rubenstein's illness had been revealed, a close friend.

He reached the end of the corridor, starting to thread his way through the evacuees and toward the doors leading to the outside.

Reed checked the Timex on his left wrist—the Russian gunships would fill the skies at any moment. From the battered flap holster hanging at his right hip, he drew the 1911A1, working the slide of the .45, jacking a round into the chamber, leaving the hammer at full stand and upping the safety.

He pushed through the inner doors, his left hand helping ease a wheelchair patient through the doors. He reached the outer doors; the guard there was directing the flow of traffic—wheelchair patients to the ramp, ambulatory patients down the steps.

Trucks were pulling up in front of the school, men pouring from the trucks to aid in the evacuation.

Above the din, the shouts, the blaring of the PA system, he heard the thrashing noise in the air.

In the distance, he could see their outlines, like huge, dark insects, like a swarm of mechanical locusts coming to devour all in their path.

He closed his eyes an instant, hammering his left fist against his thigh. Inside the improvised field hospital—Reed almost prayed Mrs. Rubenstein would die now so that her husband, his friend, might take the chance to live.

But he knew inside him that it wouldn't happen that way.

Reed stared at the helicopters—they were coming closer. He ran the fingers of his left hand through his hair. He shouted toward the sky, toward the Soviet force, "God damn you all to hell!"

But he wondered if hell could be worse than the War.

Chapter Two

Rozhdestvenskiy stood beside Comrade Professor Zlovski, lighting a cigarette despite the fact that posted everywhere throughout the laboratory were boldly lettered signs *Kureetvaspreshahyetsa*. Colonel Nehemiah Rozhdestvenskiy realized he was someone for whom signs which arbitrarily gave orders no longer possessed the slightest meaning.

He watched; the coffin shaped object's blue light seeming to flicker, the swirling clouds inside it parting, as did clouds before the dawn, he thought. And in a very real way, Rozhdestvenskiy considered, it was a dawn—the dawn of a new age for Earth.

If the man had survived.

Rozhdestvenskiy looked at Zlovski, noting the man's chin trembling slightly from the oscillation of the spear point of his little beard. "When will we know, Comrade Professor?"

"Comrade Colonel Rozhdestvenskiy—we—we shall know in a matter of seconds. The cryogenic chambers are designed to stimulate the occupant toward awakening, yet not abruptly. We—we shall know in seconds."

Rozhdestvenskiy only nodded, turning his attention back to the coffin shaped cryogenic chamber. It was one of the Soviet made chambers, but had been altered to match function for function those twelve chambers of American manufacture which had been confiscated from the ruins of the Johnson Space Center along with the ninety-six three litre bottles of the nearly clear green liquid which was the all-important serum. The subject of the cryogenic suspended animation test—Rozhdestvenskiy had memorized the man's name as a courageous hero of the Soviet Union, whether the man survived or not—had been injected with the correctly calculated amount of the cryogenic serum based upon body weight. The volunteer's name was Corporal Vassily Gurienko.

"Corporal," Rozhdestvenskiy called out. "Do you live, Corporal? Vassily?"

Inside the chamber, as the clouds of the blue cryogenic gas dissipated, there was movement.

"It could only be a reaction of the body—an autonomic response, Comrade Colonel," Zlovski cautioned.

"Vas-sil-y!"

"Comrade Colonel!"

"Vas-sil-y!"

Slowly, the body inside the chamber rose, like a figure in a child's nightmare sitting up from a coffin, the covering, the lid of the chamber elevating in perfect synchrony with the form inside. Slowly, the torso bent until Corporal Vassily Gurienko sat fully erect. The man was naked save for a light blue cloth covering over his legs, this partially dropped away, his private parts unconsciously displayed now.

Rozhdestvenskiy walked toward the cryogenic chamber. "Corporal?"

The occupant of the cryogenic chamber—his lower jaw dropped. "Comrade Colonel—I—what is—I feel—"

Rozhdestvenskiy spoke slowly. "You were born where, Corporal?"

"Minsk—Minsk, Comrade Colonel."

"Three times nine is how much?"

"Twenty-seven," the man answered after an instant's pause.

"What is the mathematical equivalent of pi?"

"Ahh—three point one four one six, Comrade Colonel."

"What are you doing here?"

"Comrade Colonel—I volunteered to serve the State,

12

Comrade Colonel—"

"How?"

"To test, Comrade Colonel, to test the cryogenic chambers which will carry ourselves of the Committee For State Security Elite Corps and the selected female comrades and the support personnel five hundred years into the future to reawaken—to reawaken and to conquer the planet and to destroy the six returning United States Space Shuttles with our particle beam defense systems before they are able to land, Comrade Colonel, and to—"

"Never mind," Rozhdestvenskiy whispered. Rozhdestvenskiy took a half step back, bringing his heels together, raising his right hand to his forehead, "I salute you, Comrade Corporal Gurienko, as a Hero of The Soviet Union."

Rozhdestvenskiy dropped the salute, turned to look at Professor Zlovski. "Well?"

"I have told you, Comrade Colonel—there is no proper test of so short a duration and—"

"The indications?"

"They are all good, Comrade Colonel—the corporal, he must be subjected to extensive medical tests before we know more and—"

Rozhdestvenskiy made a slicing motion through the air with his right hand, dropping his cigarette to the laboratory floor and heeling it out. He picked up the red telephone on the edge of the nearest lab table. "This is Rozhdestvenskiy. Give me Communications." He waited, while the connection was made, a ringing sound once, then a voice beginning a formal answering procedure. "Never mind that—this is Colonel Rozhdestvenskiy—send message seventeen. I repeat, message seventeen. Send continuously until there is response. I am in the Cryogenics Laboratory and shall be returning to my Command Center." He hung up.

"You are not curious, Comrade Professor?"

"About what, Comrade Colonel?"

Rozhdestvenskiy felt himself smiling. "Message seventeen—what it is?"

"I was not listening, Comrade Colonel—I would not presume—"

"It is a coded signal to the Kremlin Bunker—it is only one word. 'Come.' Sometimes," he nodded, starting to walk away, "one word is all that is needed. I shall wish to peruse the medical findings of the corporal's condition personally, and have you available to me all the while for consultation. See to it, Zlovski." Then Rozhdestvenskiy stopped, lighting another cigarette—he would have five centuries to break the habit. "The corporal is to be treated with the dignity which would be accorded a hero of his stature." And he smiled at the professor. "Comrade Professor Zlovski— thank you very much—a most worthwhile entertainment— most," and he walked away, listening to the click of the heels of his Italian loafers on the hard laboratory floor.

All but like the gods of Greco-Roman myth, he was immortal now.

Chapter Three

John Thomas Rourke slipped the Low Alpine Systems Loco Pack's straps over his shoulders, watching as Natalia prepared herself — at least physically — for the ordeal which remained ahead of them. The twin stainless L-Frame Metalife Custom Smiths had never left her throughout the conference with her uncle, General Varakov, in the mummy room of the museum by Lake Michigan, nor had the shoulder holster — he had found out it was a Ken Null SMZ — with the special silencer fitted stainless American Walther PPK/S. But she was slinging her two M-16s to her body now, as Rourke watched her. And there was Captain Vladov, the Soviet Special Forces Leader. One of his men had brought forth Vladov's additional gear. Other than the Smith & Wesson stainless Model 659 9mm he had worn earlier, Vladov now carried a second handgun, identical to the first. Still a third Smith & Wesson 9mm pistol he carried in what appeared to be a handmade tanker style holster, this gun the almost black looking 469, called the 'Mini' Gun before The Night of The War. The factories which produced American small arms had been occupied and in some cases made to continue production, mostly assembly from existing parts, Natalia had told him.

Rourke turned to the face of the man who had changed his destiny, or perhaps helped him to fulfill it, if indeed there were destiny at all. General Ishmael Varakov, Supreme Commander North American Army of Occupation of The Soviet.

The general still sat on his backless bench, his secretary Catherine standing beside and behind him, her left hand resting gently on the massive old man's equally massive left shoulder. The second Soviet Special Forces officer had arrived, with his men as well, a Lieutenant Daszrozinski.

General Varakov spoke. "The assault which I propose, Dr. Rourke, is the only means by which the KGB can be prevented from fulfilling its goals. But I feel a guilt that I send you all to your deaths despite this knowledge."

John Rourke checked the Gerber fighting knife he had added to his gear before leaving for Chicago. As he sheathed the black handled MkII, he spoke, "Captain Vladov has five men and Lieutenant Daszrozinski has five men—a total of twelve Russians, plus Natalia of course. If there were only thirteen Russians," he smiled, "an assault on the Womb to recover the cryogenic serum or destroy it and knock out the particle beam weapons there might be doomed to failure, I agree. But I'm an American. That'll make the difference." He watched Natalia's eyes grow wider as he spoke, their incredible, surreal blueness brighter somehow in the contrast of the dim light of the mummy room. "And, if as you proposed, General Varakov, I can get the help of U.S. II in this, well," and he laughed, "even just two or three more Americans added into—" and he paused, gesturing toward the Soviet SF-ers around him, knowing they were his allies now against the KGB, but finding it still hard to realize fully—"this assault force, well. You know what they always say. One American can lick any couple dozen people from anywhere else in the world. So, a thousand of Rozhdestvenskiy's Elite KGB Corps, the thousand women he has there to perpetuate the KGB, all the support personnel, the thousands of American small arms stored there, the millions of rounds of ammunition. All of that— well, if mankind survives somehow after the ionization effect begins and ends, well—history will probably show that this—" and he gestured again to the even dozen Soviet Special Forces troops and then to Natalia and himself— "this assault force just took advantage of those poor misguided

KGB people."

Natalia Anastasia Tiemerovna began to laugh, hysterically, doubling forward with it, holding the M-16s back on their slings, falling to her knees. And suddenly, Captain Vladov, whom Varakov himself had labelled the best soldier in the Soviet Union, began to laugh, Lieutenant Daszrozinski joining him, the sergeants each man had, the enlisted personnel laughing, too.

Catherine, Varakov's secretary with the too-long uniform skirt, smiled. Varakov, his face seaming, began to laugh, a laugh that sounded like a child's dream of Santa Claus as it rolled sonorously from his massive body.

John Rourke began to check one, then the other of the twin stainless Detonics Combat Master .45s he wore—it was the first time in his life, he smiled, that he had ever been funny. And in view of what lay before them, he thought, most likely the last time as well.

Chapter Four

Dawn came — the world had not perished by fire as it would, perhaps the next sunrise, or the next. It was an indefinite sentence of death — sometime, some sunrise within the next seven days at best, because of the electrically charged particles which had been thrust into the atmosphere during the bombings and missile strikes of The Night of The War, the total ionization of the atmosphere would take place. The atmosphere would catch fire, the fire spreading as the electrically charged particles were acted upon by the sun. It would be the last sunrise for humanity. As the earth rotated and the sun eventually rose throughout the twenty-four hours, there would be twenty-four hours of death, the sky itself aflame, the surface of the earth destroyed, the atmosphere all but completely burned away, much of the ozone layer destroyed. Humanity and all the lower life forms would be obliterated — forever.

And General Varakov had held out one chance — that in a hermetically sealed shelter such as Rourke's own survival Retreat in the mountains of northeast Georgia not far from the town of Helen, his wife Sarah, his son Michael and his daughter Annie could survive, and that he — Rourke — could survive as well, and so could Natalia and Paul Rubenstein and any others the Retreat could accommodate. All through the use of the cryogenic chambers originally developed for deep space travel, in use with the six craft of the Space Shuttle Fleet somewhere on an elliptical voyage to the end of the solar system and back. The cryogenic sleep chambers, coupled with the almost mystical serum which allowed the human brain to be awakened from the life sustaining, unaging sleep, could allow Rourke's family to survive the scorching of the earth and the sky, to survive the centuries while the lower plant forms gradually rebuilt the atmosphere to a level comparable to the highest altitude mountain atmospheres—but liveable. The chambers and the serum without which the chambers would be a perpetual living death from which there could be no awakening would allow his family to awaken five centuries in the future to a world, once again and however marginally, habitable. And to awaken to the hoped for return of the Eden Project survivors, an international corps of deep space astronaut trainees recruited because of their skills and their physical perfection from all the western aligned nations. To return with their microfilm libraries of the accumulated knowledge of mankind, their cryogenically frozen embryonic life forms—domestic animals, livestock, even birds to sing again in the air if indeed there were air.

An Ark.

But Colonel Nehemiah Rozhdestvenskiy, successor to Vladmir Karamatsov, the husband of Major Natalia Tiemerovna whom John Rourke had killed in a standup gunfight engineered by Natalia's uncle General Varakov, had assembled the one thousand finest of his Elite KGB Corps. With one thousand handpicked perfect Soviet female specimens, with the secret of life sustaining cryogenic sleep stolen with the American cryogenic serum, they would survive the global holocaust to use particle beam weapons already installed at what once had been NORAD Headquarters at Cheyenne Mountain, Colorado, they would survive in what Rozhdestvenskiy had dubbed "The Womb" to destroy the returning Eden Project before the last survivors of the world democracies could land, could reclaim the purged earth.

It was this that was his mission, John Rourke realized, sitting in the semi-darkness at the height of the mezzanine steps, but in shadow from the first floor of the museum itself. He could see the two figures of mastodons fighting. Natalia had told him how her uncle watched these without cease. He understood the reason—and like the mastodons, he was now prepared to fight unto extinction because the circumstances of his own life had issued him no choice. It was his mission, above the saving of his wife and children, beyond saving Natalia and Paul and even himself for a world five centuries from now—it was his mission to prevent the KGB Elite Corps from utilizing the cryogenic serum, destroy the particle beam weapons, prevent the ultimate Soviet domination of the entire earth, the ultimate victory for evil.

It was an involuntary nerve response, a paroxysm, the shiver which ran along his spine—as a doctor he could think of a multiplicity of medical related reasons for it. But the truest reason was within himself and what he had to do.

Chapter Five

Sarah Rourke, wearing a borrowed sweater—Natalia's things fit her almost perfectly—and her own blue denim skirt, the only skirt she owned, sat on one of the high rocks not far from the Retreat entrance, her pistol in its holster on the ground beside her. On the next rock, Paul Rubenstein sat, an M-16 across his lap, some kind of submachinegun slung diagonally across his back, a pistol—she recognized it as a Browning High Power—in a shoulder holster that positioned the pistol half across the left side of his chest.

"Are you sure you're well enough—"

"It was only my left arm, Mrs. Rourke—I shoot with my right—"

"I didn't mean that—and it's Sarah—"

"Sarah," he nodded, pushing his wire-rimmed glasses up off the bridge of his nose with his right index finger. "Anyway, the fresh air's good for me."

"Do you think the children—"

"I left a note on the pillow next to Michael—he can read it, know we're just outside—I just—" And he looked at her. "Why'd you come out here? John tell you to keep an eye on me with my arm?"

She shook her head—it was such a good feeling to have clean hair, to wash it with seemingly limitless hot water. She suddenly wondered—shivering—what it would be like when all the supplies stored in the shelves and cabinets of her husband's Retreat were depleted. She had looked through the library—there were books which showed how to weave cloth, books which showed how to make soap from animal fat. Would they someday wear rags? Live by the light of homemade candles because the supply of light bulbs and fluorescent tubes had been depleted—she laughed at the irony. Limitless electricity from the hydro-electric generators her husband had installed—but electricity was useless without lights. She laughed—out loud—"I'm sorry—"

"What is it?" Paul Rubenstein asked her.

"Nothing—I was just thinking—how stupid I'll feel someday running around in rags or animals skins cooking wild rabbit by candlelight on a microwave oven."

Paul Rubenstein started to laugh and she laughed with him. It was nice to have something to look forward to, after all, Sarah Rourke thought.

Chapter Six

He had taken an M-16 from a soldier killed in the first pass the helicopters had made across the school grounds. As the machines banked, their guns opening up again, plowing waves in the dirt on both sides of the disabled, already burning truck behind which he had taken cover, Reed leveled the assault rifle toward the bubble dome of the nearest of the machines—they were American Bell 209 Huey Cobras, taken over by the Russians, a red Soviet star emblazoned over the American markings. Reed squeezed the trigger, firing, emptying the M-16's magazine, the helicopter's 7.62mm multi-barrel Minigun still firing, the helicopter unswerving, unaffected.

"Shit!"

He tucked down, the ground on both sides of the truck erupting as another of the machines made a pass, the sound of bullets ricocheting off the metal of the truck body. Screams—not all of the patients had been successfully evacuated from the building and those that were, were still pinned down in the trucks, some at the far end of the road, others still in front of the school.

The sound of a missile firing—Reed looked up. The contrail, then one of the two and a half ton trucks at the far edge of the driveway seemed to bounce upward for an instant, then was consumed in a ball of flame. Men, women, their clothes and hair afire, fell from the back of the truck.

"Bastards!" Reed screamed at the machines as they finished the pass. They were coming back.

For some reason he turned around—he had never believed in a sixth sense beyond the uneasy feeling one sometimes got in combat. But Colonel Rubenstein had left the school building. The man stood there. He screamed, "My wife is dead!" His hands tore at the collar of his shirt, ripping it. Suddenly, Reed was conscious of Rubenstein being a Jew and Reed seemed to remember that the rending of some article of clothing was a tradition for the death of a loved one.

Reed started to shout, "I'm sorry." But then the school steps vaporized in a ball of flame and Colonel Rubenstein was gone.

Reed stabbed the M-16 skyward, firing it out uselessly, screaming the word again and again, "Bastards!"

He pushed himself to his feet, out of magazines for the M-16, running toward the nearest of the trucks which could still move, shouting toward the cab, "Driver—get us out of here!"

As he started to climb aboard, hanging on to the stakes that surrounded the truck bed, he realized the truck's engine was not running. "Driver!"

His .45 in his fist, Reed jumped to the ground. Screams of the wounded and dying were drowned out by the rattle of machinegun fire, the long staccato pulse that sounded like a solitary drone of some huge wasp as it beat its wings. The truck beside him was hit, Reed throwing himself to the dirt and gravel of the driveway, a shower of the material of the driveway raining down on him.

Flames engulfed the truck beside him—screams, bodies on fire hurtling themselves from the vehicle.

A missile impacted the front of the school, flames now belching from the roof as he pulled himself to his feet. He climbed up into the truck cab—the windshield was peppered with spiderwebbed bullet holes—the driver's eyes were wide open in death, the front of the fatigue blouse dark and wet with blood.

Reed shoved the body through the driver's side door, "God bless you, son," he murmured, starting the deuce and a half. "Hang on back there," Reed shouted behind him. "Hang on!" The sick, the wounded—he didn't want to add them to the ranks of the dead.

He pumped the clutch, stomping the gas pedal, letting the truck start rolling forward, the gunships coming through for another pass. One of the helicopters was coming right at him as he upshifted, cranking the wheel hard left and out of the driveway. Reed ducked, machinegun fire blowing out the window—he was losing control of the truck—losing it. As he moved on the seat, he could feel the shards of glass falling, hear the tinkle of glass as it fell from his clothes, breaking, feel the crunch of it under and around him. He fought the wheel, trying to get control. A tree—he cut the wheel hard right. He felt it as he threw himself down, the lurch, the tremor of the truck cab around him, the shuddering of his own body as he slammed forward and rolled from the seat, his right elbow hitting the driveshaft hump, his head striking the dashboard.

With his left hand he felt for the door handle, twisting at it, his right hand clutching for the cocked and locked .45 which was back in his holster. He found it, half falling from the truck cab to the ground, steam rising in a whistling column from where the nose of the deuce and a half had struck the tree.

Reed staggered, falling to his knees, still clutching the .45.

He looked skyward—the Soviet marked gunships were breaking off, disengaging.

Reed looked around him now—the school was awash with flames, all but two of the trucks burning or otherwise disabled.

Bodies lay everywhere about the driveway, moans of the dying filling the air as the beating of the helicopter rotor blades died on the air slowly.

Reed got to his feet. His left hand was bleeding, he realized, and his head ached badly.

He staggered toward the rear of the truck, ripping back the tarpaulin cover there.

"Jesus." He turned away, feeling the thing in the pit of his stomach, gagging as the vomit rose in him, falling to his knees as it poured from his mouth onto the ground.

The twenty or so people in the back of the truck were all dead.

He set down his pistol just to the side of the puddle of vomit, his left elbow aching as he moved the arm, both hands finding the lapel of his fatigue blouse. For Colonel Rubenstein, for Mrs. Rubenstein—for all the dead. It was hard to tear the fabric, but on the third try, it ripped.

Chapter Seven

Natalia Anastasia Tiemerovna, Major, Committee for State Security of The Soviet, felt the warmth and strength of her uncle's arms around her, a warmth and strength she had felt and loved since she was a little child, something she would never know again. She tasted the salt of her own tears mingled with the salt of General Ishmael Varakov's tears as her head rested against his chest. "All — all of it — in the letter to John Rourke — about my real parents — my real mother — it — it only made me love you more, Uncle Ishmael — it only —"

"I told all of those things in the letter because I thought perhaps, child, that I might never see you again, and you had the right to know these things. How goes it with the American Rourke?"

She still let her uncle hold her, there in the quiet darkness of the mummy room. "He has found his wife and children, Uncle —"

"What of you, child?"

She closed her eyes so tight she could see red and green floaters in them.

"What of you, child?"

"She knows — his wife knows that I love him. And that he loves me — he actually loves me."

"A man does not have two wives — at least not a man like this Dr. John Rourke."

"We — we —"

"Perhaps he thinks of the Jew, Rubenstein, of him for you should the Eden Project not return —"

She kept her eyes closed. "I love Paul — but like he were

27

my brother, Uncle—like that only. I would rather go on loving John Rourke and have him never touch me than to lie that I could love someone else."

"She is older than you?"

"She is thirty-two, perhaps thirty-three, I think, there is only four or five years of difference between us—"

"Then you will both outlive him if you somehow survive this holocaust."

"I would not want—"

"To live if this Rourke man were dead?"

"Yes—I would not."

"You are skilled in many ways, child—"

She closed her eyes still tighter, like she had when Karamatsov had beaten her before Rourke had killed him. "I could never—it would—it would be—"

"I know that you could never," and she felt his body shudder as he laughed. "The efficient KGB killing machine— you were called that once and I never told you. A killing machine in skirts and silk stockings—a member of the Politburo spoke of you that way when you and Karamatsov worked together in Latin America before The Night of The War. But I knew that what the Politburo member said was wrong. Your heart—it has always been the heart of your real mother—did I tell you in the letter that her name was Natalia as well?"

"Yes—yes, Uncle," she whispered. "You told me that—"

"An old man forgets, child. But there are some things— some things that an old man can never—" He ceased to speak.

"Forget," she whispered for him.

"There are some things, and perhaps for you John Rourke is such a thing—would that she had so worshiped me as is evident you worship this Rourke—"

"He is—"

He released his arms from her, turning up her chin with the tips of the fingers of both his massive, spatulate hands.

"He is a man—"

"He is more, Uncle—he—"

"I am not a religious person—but it is wrong to speak of such things, I think. For a man to worship a woman, or a woman to worship a man—this can be. But—but he is not your god. Perhaps, child," and she looked into his eyes, tear-rimmed, large, loving seeming to her, "—perhaps, child, neither you nor I can have a god. And if in the hour of my death, I should discover one, it will be the same one that someday perhaps you shall discover, and Dr. Rourke shall discover too. And your John Rourke—he will not discover his god by staring at his own image in a reflecting pool and being deceived. It is in this Rourke's eyes—that he is not this sort of man. If you love him so, then respect him also for what he is and what he is not and would never pretend to be."

She closed her eyes again, hugging her arms as best she could around her uncle's chest—and it was something unchanging since she had been a little girl—her fingertips would not meet no matter how hard she tried, how tightly she squeezed . . .

Chapter Eight

If free will were in its exercise an intrinsic good, then those who would consciously and totally abrogate the exercise of free will for the bulk of mankind for their own purposes were, by contrast, intrinsically evil.

Good. Evil.

Rourke considered these as he stood at the height of the mezzanine steps, staring down at Varkov's figures of the mastodons which dominated the museum hall. John Rourke looked at the Rolex Submariner on his left wrist. Varakov indicated they would have to be clear of the museum by eight forty-five at the latest. It was almost eight-thirty. But the thought of rushing Natalia's last farewell to her uncle, though it entered his mind, was something Rourke instantaneously dismissed.

He had removed his pack again, placing it on one of the benches at the rear of the mezzanine, his M-16 beside it, only the CAR-15 slung cross body from his left shoulder under his right arm now. He looked back, hearing footsteps.

It was Natalia, walking slowly beside her uncle.

Rourke turned back toward the great hall, whistling low, once, Vladov's man beside the brass doors leading to the outside turning, acknowledging.

Rourke turned back to stare at Natalia. As he did, he spoke to Vladov, on the mezzanine beside him. "Captain, looks like we're ready."

"It would appear so, Dr. Rourke."

"How do you feel about this — going against other Russians like yourself?"

"At the Womb?"

"Yes, at the Womb?"

"They are other Russians—but they are not like myself."

Rourke looked at the man. "Fair enough," Rourke nodded deliberately. He turned back to Natalia, watching. Varakov, beside her, stopped as he reached the edge of the mezzanine.

Rourke listened as the old man spoke. "It is time, child."

Natalia only nodded, her face turned down, as if staring at her uncle's feet or her own.

Rourke stepped forward toward them, his left arm folding around her shoulders. He extended his right hand. "General Varakov, I think we could have been friends if all of us hadn't been so bent on butchering each other, sir."

Varakov took his hand—the grip was warm, firm, exuding strength. "I think that you are quite correct, Dr. Rourke. You will care for her—"

"Like my own life, sir—more than that."

"I trust you and you alone with the greatest joy of my life."

Rourke nodded, almost whispering, "I know that, sir." Their hands were still clasped.

"We Communists are taught that there is no God to believe in—like Marx spoke of. But in the event we have been wrong all these decades since we attempted to liberate man from his chains, then I wish that God—if He exists—bless you all and protect you."

"We capitalists are taught," Rourke smiled, "that hedging your bet is never a bad thing, General. May God bless you, too."

The old man nodded, his eyes lit with something Rourke could not read, but something somehow Rourke could understand. They released each other's grips.

Varakov folded Natalia into his arms, speaking to her in Russian. "I love you—you are the daughter, you are the life I never led. Kiss me good-bye, child—forever."

31

Rourke closed his eyes, opening them as Natalia moved into her uncle's arms, then turning away.

He heard her voice behind him, in English, saying, "I'm ready, John."

Rourke turned back. Varakov stared, past him. Rourke looked behind him. Captain Vladov and Lieutenant Daszrozsinski stood at stiff attention, right hands raised in salute.

As he looked back to Varakov, the old man, his uniform tunic open, his shoes unlaced, his shirt collar open, returned the salute sharply. "God — if He hears me and if He is there to begin with — God speed."

As Rourke drew Natalia to him, he said only one word. "Sir."

Chapter Nine

Across the profile of Vladov's AKS-74 assault rifle, as John Rourke looked at him where they stood beside the massive brass doors, Rourke could see tears rimming the Soviet Special Forces captain's eyes.

Rourke looked at Natalia—she was staring behind them, and Rourke looked back then once. Varakov, his secretary Catherine beside him, stood at the balcony of the mezzanine, only staring.

Rourke rasped, "Let's go—our best tribute to him is to do what the general called us here for—Captain?"

"Agreed," the man nodded, licking his lips.

"Natalia?"

She stared at him, her blue eyes awash with tears. Then she nodded, "Yes," and pushed through the crack between the doors, Rourke right behind her.

The sun was higher over the lake than Rourke would have supposed, but it had been a long time since he had seen a Chicago sunrise. Thunder rumbled in the sky to the east as Rourke, a step behind Natalia, his M-16 in his hands, raced down the museum steps, diagonally, and toward the lanes of Lake Shore Drive which cut between the museum and the aquarium and the planetarium beyond, the click of the Soviet Special Forces troopers' boots on the stone steps loud and oddly reassuring. Rourke shot a glance at his Rolex, the cuff of his bomber jacket already rolled back—it was eight forty-two. At eight forty-five for some reason Varakov had not specified, there could be trouble.

Natalia sprinted ahead, toward Lake Shore Drive, no traffic there—nothing as she ducked under the horizontal

33

safety lines and into the street. Rourke followed her, hearing Vladov snap from behind him, "Look there, Dr. Rourke—from the south!"

Rourke drew up to his full height—coming up Lake Shore Drive now from the south was first one, then another, then another, and he imagined still more behind—trucks. "KGB," Vladov murmured.

Rourke looked ahead—Natalia was nearly across the drive. Rourke broke into a dead run behind her, rasping, "Come on, Vladov!" His M-16 at high port, the CAR-15 banging against his side as he ran, Rourke reached the far side of the drive, Natalia still sprinting ahead, crossing beyond the sidewalk and onto the grass, heading toward the lake side of the spit of land beyond the aquarium, roadway, parkway strip, then roadway and more parkway, then finally the lake to Rourke's right. But the shelter of the rocks was beyond the aquarium. "Come on," Rourke shouted. "Hurry—follow Major Tiemerovna!" Rourke picked up his run, glancing once to his right and behind him—the trucks, KGB personnel on motorcycles flanking them—he could recognize them by the green tabs of their uniforms. He hit the grass, running alongside the aquarium now, Natalia disappearing behind the aquarium, Rourke running after her.

Rourke reached the back end of the building, taking a quick left behind it, running. Ahead the ground dropped off, Rourke reaching the edge, remembering what lay beyond well enough not to jump for it. But he flipped down, picking his landing spot in the instant before he moved, missing an eight-inch wide crack between the slabs of tan colored natural rock and chunks of concrete which formed the low sea wall against the Lake Michigan waters. He ducked down, Natalia already there, one of her M-16s up, ready.

Vladov was the first of the SF-ers down, then Lieutenant Daszrozinski and like something choreographed, one after the other, the remaining ten Soviet SF-ers.

"What do we do, Comrade Major?" Vladov asked, sounding slightly out of breath. Rourke couldn't be certain, but the pounding in his own chest led him to the conclusion. "Do we wait here or proceed?"

"Those trucks," Natalia panted. "They—they are heading for Meiggs Field?"

"Yes, Comrade Major. Each day the KGB have been shipping out supplies by nine-fifteen—we do not know what."

"How big are the planes they use?" Rourke interrupted.

"They are American Boeing KC-135Bs."

Rourke nodded, thinking. "There were steel mills beyond the bend in the shoreline—could be billets of steel—maybe Rozhdestvenskiy wants some laid in at the Womb to handle early construction after the awakening."

"Perhaps," Natalia mused. "There were also automotive assembly plants—perhaps engine parts."

"Whatever the hell it is, what do you think?" Rourke asked her, his voice low. "You know the KGB better than any of us."

He watched her eyes. "My uncle has the boats waiting just beyond the planetarium. Some of the GRU men he trusted are with them, but they are not insane. If we wait and do not make our rendezvous—" and he saw her eye the gold ladies Rolex she wore on her wrist for an instant— "they will leave and we will be stranded here."

"No choice for it then," and Rourke turned to Vladov. "Have your men keep low and have 'em watch their footing. We'll follow this out all the way to the land's end—"

"Agreed," Vladov nodded, saying to his men, "As the doctor has said—keep low—be careful of your footing among these rocks—we follow the major and Doctor Rourke."

Natalia started up from her knees, Rourke grabbing at her right forearm, looking at her for an instant. "I'm sorry—sorry this had to happen. All of it—except meeting you."

35

"I as well—except for that," and she pulled away from him, breaking into a crouching run along the rocks, Rourke after her.

Chapter Ten

Sam Chambers, president of U.S. II spoke slowly. "This is butchery—pure butchery—"

Reed closed his eyes, inhaling on his cigarette, slowly saying to the president, "It proves what I've been saying, Mr. President—a major Soviet offensive directed against us. They're softening us up. That's why they did this. Demoralize us. For the last two weeks at least, there've been all the signs. Airborne reconnaissance shows units of the Army and KGB units too massing in east Texas and in central Louisiana. They're going to bite us right between 'em—"

Reed looked at Chambers—it was better than surveying the bodies in the elementary school driveway, better than watching the few surviving medics working with those who weren't quite dead yet. Chambers' helicopter's rotor blades beat slowly, rhythmically at the far side of the drive. Then Chambers spoke. "Your efforts to contact the reorganized Texas volunteer militia—"

"I don't know, sir. I sent Lieutenant Feltcher out three weeks ago—we haven't heard from him since. If he did make contact, they could have killed him as a spy—I don't know. Since the death of Randan Soames, the leadership has changed at least a half-dozen times—could have been infiltrated with more of the Communists—we don't know. And there were the rumors some of the larger brigand bands had formed some sort of alliance with the militia. We just don't know, sir."

"But they're the only hope we have, aren't they, Reed—"

Reed nodded, dropping his cigarette to the gravel, heeling it out. Suddenly the nausea passed over him again—

stuck to a piece of the gravel near his boot was what looked like a pink piece of human flesh, burned at the edges. He breathed deeply, to make the feeling pass, then tried to answer. "If they come and link up with us before the Russians strike—somehow—then we can beat this Russian force. If they get caught up with the Russians in east Texas, then we can take on the Russians in central Louisiana. If they don't come at all, it's either surrender or be crushed. It'd be a slaughter."

"We won't surrender," Chambers said firmly.

"I didn't think we would, sir," Reed told him. Because there were other members of the civilian cabinet nearby, and some younger officers as well, Reed didn't add that all surrender would mean was a firing squad or worse. It was better to die standing up, fighting for what you believed in.

Reed lit another cigarette—where the hell was Feltcher, he thought. Had he reached the Texas Volunteer Militia or just died trying?

Chapter Eleven

They had reached land's end, the lapping of the waves loud against the rocks beneath them; Rourke peered round the rock border along which they had moved, seeing three six-man Avon rubber boats, the kind divers sometimes used. All three boats, fitted with impressively large outboard motors, were moored to the rocks, a solitary man holding an AK-47 standing guard beside them, using the wooden buttstock of the AK to push the boats away from the rocks when the waves forced them too close. Two other men stood further in on the rocks, away from the Avon inflatables, AK-47s at the ready position.

Rourke turned back to Natalia, using hand signals to reveal his findings. She nodded, murmuring the three letters, "GRU." Rourke nodded. Natalia peered around the edge of the rocks for a moment, then looked back at Rourke. She repeated the three initials, "GRU," then stood up, the rocks shielding her from view further back along the land.

He watched as she stepped—slowly—from behind the rocks, her voice a low whisper, "I am Major Tiemerovna, gentlemen. You wait for me."

Rourke followed after her, the Soviet SF-ers behind him. The GRU man beside the three rubber boats didn't even turn around, but one of the other two did, the man nearest them. He brought his AK-47 to present arms, "Comrade Major Tiemerovna—it is an honor." She only nodded, her hair caught up in the wind now off the lake, her left hand, unconsciously it seemed, but gracefully pushing the dark, almost black strands back from her face.

"You are ready for our departure?" she asked, Rourke

leaning now against the rocks, partially blocking her from the GRU man who had saluted and spoken to her. It was still difficult to trust a self-proclaimed Soviet agent. Yet he realized the absurdity of it — he trusted Natalia with his life.

"Yes, Comrade Major — but the outboard engines — they are loud. If the KGB should hear they could open fire at us — these are only rubber boats and not bullet resistant."

"I'll take a look," Rourke interjected quietly. He handed over his M-16 to Natalia, pushing the scoped CAR-15 back further along his body, starting up the rocks to get his head even with the level of the land above. It took only a few seconds for Rourke to reach the level of the land above. Slowly, he raised his head to peer across the spit of land. The trucks were in full view now, the motorcycle personnel attending them parked at the perimeter of the airfield to his far left.

But driving slowly along the spit of land was a vehicle, coming toward the planetarium.

He didn't know why.

He ducked back down, clambering down from the rocks, standing beside Natalia again, rasping to her, "There's a car coming — they've got a radio antenna — one of the converted Chicago PD cars — "

"That is a patrol — this area is patrolled regularly — we have waited too long," the GRU man who had spoken earlier declared. "We are trapped here. There will be three men. There always are — usually they are only two man patrols but by the lakeside they use three. They will exit the car and come down here to look — one of them always urinates over the side of the rocks."

"Wonderful," Rourke barely whispered.

"We cannot run the outboard motors — they would hear us — "

"Then we kill 'em," Rourke shrugged. "Before they can use their radio and get any of the troops by the airfield over here."

"But there is no time," the GRU man said. "Soon, the planes from the field will be taking off. If we are not well away from here, we will be spotted by one of the cargo pilots. And we cannot hug the shoreline—the coastal watchers."

"Sounds like a marvelous plan you guys had," Rourke commented drily. "Then we take those guys out quick—get everyone away in two of the boats and leave the last boat for those of us who take out the three KGB patrolmen." He looked at Natalia. "I'd like to say we'll do this together, but one of the two of us has to get away—otherwise there's no chance for Sarah and the children, for Paul—"

"I will stay," Natalia announced. "I will stay."

"I knew you'd say that," Rourke nodded, his right hand flashing up, the knuckles catching the tip of her chin, his left arm scooping out, catching her as she sagged back limply, her eyelids fluttering, then closed.

"You struck the major!" the GRU man snapped.

It was Captain Vladov who interceded. "He struck the major in order to save her life."

"Doesn't matter how tough a woman is," Rourke commented, sweeping Natalia up into his arms and starting toward the nearest of the three Avon inflatables, carrying her. "Almost always count on 'em to have glass jaws—"

"A jaw of glass?" the GRU man asked, puzzled sounding.

"Old American expression," Rourke told him. Then he looked at Lieutenant Daszrozinski. "Lieutenant, get some of your men down into this boat so I can hand the major down to you. If it's all right with Captain Vladov, he and I can stay behind with one other man and take out those KGB patrolmen." And Rourke looked at the only one of the three GRU men who had yet spoken. "One of your guys stays behind to keep the boat ready—and as soon as we do what we have to do, signal the other two boats to start their engines and make time."

41

"Make the time?"

"Go fast," Rourke explained.

"I will stay," the GRU man said.

"Good," Rourke nodded. Daszrozinski and two other men had already climbed down from the rocks into the nearest of the Avon rubber boats—and Rourke began handing Natalia into Daszrozinski's and a second man's arms. "When the major wakes up, well, tell her not to be mad at me, huh?"

Daszrozinski's very Slavik, red-cheeked face showed a grin. "I will try my best, Dr. Rourke."

Rourke nodded, "Right."

He turned to Vladov—already Vladov had one of the men beside him—a corporal. "Corporal Ravitski will assist us, Dr. Rourke."

Rourke nodded

"May I suggest a plan, Dr. Rourke?"

"Certainly, Captain," Rourke agreed. Already, the first of the rubber boats was pushing off, the second loading. Rourke looked once more after Natalia.

Chapter Twelve

She knew what he had done as soon as she opened her eyes, the light hurting for an instant as she squeezed them closed against it. He had done it so expertly that aside from a little tenderness as she moved her jaw, there was no pain. Her teeth felt fine.

The spray pelted at her as she sat up, Lieutenant Daszrozinski smiling at her, "Comrade Major, the doctor and Captain Vladov and one other man are seeing to the KGB patrol — one of the GRU men waits with them with the third boat. He will signal when we can start our engines."

She didn't say anything, but sat up, feeling slightly ridiculous that Rourke had — she remembered the expression, the Americanism — "cold-cocked" her so easily.

"What is their plan, Lieutenant Daszrozinski?" she finally asked him.

"I do not know, Comrade Major, but the comrade general has told Captain Vladov that Dr. Rourke is extremely competent in these matters, and, of course, Captain Vladov himself is a veteran of many such missions and —"

"Yes — enough, Lieutenant," and she dismissed listening to him. She could make out the police car, the red star emblazoned over the lakeside door, the door open. But detail beyond that from where she sat in the boat was impossible. If the plan were going well, or going badly, she could not tell.

She could only sit in the rubber boat and wait while the enlisted Special Forces personnel paddled the boat against the lake swells. At any moment, the occupants of the police car would look out onto the lake and see her craft and the companion vessel, she knew. They would start shooting. Better than two hundred meters off shore, she realized their marksmanship would have little effect. Maximum effective range of the AKM—what the KGB patrols were armed with—was three hundred meters on full auto, four hundred meters semi-automatic mode. But it took an exceptional marksman to be effective at such a range. Had the men been exceptional marksmen, they would have been assigned other duties. Hence, logically, she was in no danger.

But Rourke—the man she loved, all she had left in the world now after making her final good-byes to her uncle—Rourke was much closer than four hundred meters, or three hundred meters. He could very easily be killed by even an indifferent marksman. She realized she was wringing her hands. She turned to one of the enlisted men near her, telling him in Russian, "Move aside, I wish to help to propel the rubber boat," and she took the paddle from him before the man could protest.

It was something to do, at least.

Chapter Thirteen

He had raced along the rocks of the sea wall built against
the lake waves which could run to heights as high as sixteen
feet, the air temperature cold, his breath coming in short
puffs, but the air fresh, clean. He had positioned himself on
the far side of the planetarium, behind the police car. And
Rourke waited now, watching as the three KGB patrolmen
exited the police car, one from the front passenger seat, one
from the driver's side, one from the rear passenger compartment behind the driver's side, only two of the men carrying assault rifles, but all three wearing pistols in military
flap holsters on their belts.

If he had had Natalia's silenced Walther, he reflected, but
he did not.

The three men started walking toward the end of the spit
of land jutting out into the lake, across the grass that had
once been green, then along the circular parking area disappearing behind the planetarium. No longer able to see
them, they could no longer see him, and Rourke, eyeing the
roadway leading from Lake Shore Drive and the airfield as
well—no one was coming—pushed himself up, taking the
steps from the lower rocky walkway to the planetarium
level three at a time in a long strided run, the M-16 and the
CAR-15 left behind with Vladov and Corporal Ravitski, the
long bladed Gerber MkII in his right fist as he followed the
men.

Ravitski's job was the most unpleasant—to take out the
man who regularly urinated over the side of the sea wall.
For the purpose, he had long handled wire cutters he had
taken from the side of his backpack.

Vladov was to back him up.

Rourke kept running, the Gerber ahead of him in a fencer's hold, his black combat booted feet soundless as he raced along the pavement of the walkway, finally reaching the far wall of the planetarium, hugging against it, able to see the three KGB men again. He was to await the cut from Ravitski.

He saw the center of the three KGB-ers, arching his body slightly forward, one of the others laughing. The one about to urinate was one of the two armed with an AKM and the assault rifle was slung across his back. The one who had laughed was speaking animatedly, Rourke unable to follow the conversation because of the keening sound of the wind off the lake.

Rourke waited, ready to move, the Gerber ready in his balled right fist, his left hand palming the black chrome Sting IA from its sheath behind his left hipbone inside the waistband of his faded blue Levis.

He waited, both knives ready for their work.

The man with the fixation to empty his kidneys took two steps forward, toward the sea wall, the other two men—the one still laughing—turning their backs as he bent forward.

There was a scream, in Russian the man who had been about to urinate shouting, "My penis—" The body sagged forward.

Ravitski's long handled wire cutters had done their grisly work.

The two men—as Vladov had anticipated and Rourke had agreed—turned back, reaching out, groping toward the sea wall to snatch at the body of their stricken comrade.

Rourke threw his body into a dead run, across the once living grass, leaping, airborne, coming down on his feet, his knees buckling to take the force of the fall, throwing himself forward into a dead run, the Gerber reaching out, the spear pointed tip thrusting into the back of the man to his right, severing the spinal cord he hoped.

46

He left the knife there, the second man starting to turn, the pistol coming into his hand as Rourke's left hand punched forward, the point of the little Sting IA black chrome puncturing the adam's apple, cutting through, the man's eyes wide open, no voice box left with which to scream.

Vladov was up from the sea wall beyond, his fighting knife — a bastardized Bowie pattern, custom made, Rourke had surmised — hacking left to right across the throat of the man Rourke had stabbed with the big Gerber, severing the carotid artery and slicing through the voice box before there could be a scream.

Rourke's hands were moving — the man with the little A.G. Russell knife in his throat, Rourke's right hand thrusting upward, palm outward, open, the base of his hand impacting the base of the man's nose, punching the bone upward, through the ethmoid bone and into the brain, his left hand ripping the knife downward through the adam's apple and locking against the bone beneath the hollow of the throat.

Rourke ripped the knife free, turning as Vladov guided the other man to the ground.

As Vladov wiped his blade clean on the man's clothing, Rourke drew his own knife — the Gerber — clear.

They had killed each man at least twice to be sure.

From the converted police car, Rourke could hear a radio call.

"It is KGB headquarters — perhaps a routine radio check — "

"Let's get the hell out of here — have the GRU man give the signal."

"It is already done, I think," Vladov nodded, sheathing the Bowie pattern knife to his equipment belt, flipping down over the sea wall to the rocks below.

Rourke followed after him. In the distance, as he impacted the rocks on the soles of his boots, he could hear the drone of the outboard motors, already started up.

Rourke glanced at Corporal Ravitski—the young Russian SF-er's face was white. He looked at the man's hands—the massive wire cutters, stuck into the apex of the blade halves were something unmistakable as a human organ.

Rourke's eyes drifted downward—at the man's feet was the third KGB patrolman, blood oozing through lifeless fingers clamped over his crotch.

He would have been dead in seconds from hemorrhage, Rourke realized—but Ravitski too had taken no chances—the front of the throat was hacked open, little blood there. Perhaps the heart had already stopped pumping from shock.

A Bowie pattern bayonet for an AKM—he imagined it worked with the AKS-74 the corporal had slung across his back—lay blood smeared beside the KGB man.

Vladov took two steps and was beside the young corporal. "Andreyev, you have done your duty."

"Comrade Captain, this man was a Russian—"

"Hard tasks await us, Andreyev—hard tasks which perhaps when compared will make this task you have so efficiently performed seem easy."

"Comrade Captain—I—"

Rourke, his voice a low whisper, said, "Look, boy, that you didn't like doing this is to your credit, that you could still do it anyway is more to your credit. But it's time to move out."

The young Russian corporal turned to face him, staring. "Yes, Doctor—it is—"

"Time to move," Rourke said again.

And Rourke didn't wait, jumping down into the inflatable as it heaved toward the rocks, his M-16 and his CAR-15 already soaked with spray.

He made a mental note to clean them as Vladov and Corporal Ravitski joined him in the boat.

The GRU man tugged clear his line. In the distance

Rourke could hear the sound of aircraft engines revving, from the field, he realized — but there was no sound of police sirens — at least not yet.

John Rourke silently wondered how many more of humankind would lose their innocence in the few days humankind had remaining. Too many, he thought.

Chapter Fourteen

Soviet personnel were everywhere, Rourke imagined sparked by the wild chase the previous night through the Chicago expressway system and along underground Wacker Drive, and of course the murders of the three KGB patrolmen at the lake that morning. After ditching the rubber boats in what remained of Belmont Harbor and transferring to a medium-sized cabin cruiser, they had gone out farther into the lake. There had been a tense moment—a Soviet patrol boat. But Vladov was prepared for this—orders from the KGB, forged, given him by General Varakov. The patrol boat had passed, but as a precautionary measure Vladov had ordered the GRU pilot to change course, dangerously hugging the shoreline.

It had been late afternoon by the time they had pulled ashore near Waukegan, factory complexes—abandoned now—littering the shoreline.

Working in two teams—fire and maneuver—they had worked their way through the factory complex and into the streets of Waukegan proper, continuing the two team movement, the process slow.

The sunset was purple, the haze almost something Rourke could taste on the air as he knocked on the rear door of the American field hospital which was in reality Resistance headquarters for northern Illinois and southern Wisconsin, as he had learned earlier.

The hole in the back door of Waukegan Outdoor Sportsman opened, a face peering through, back lit. "Tell Tom Maus Major Tiemerovna and I are back to see him—I'm John Rourke."

"Wait a minute," and the peephole in the door was closed.

Rourke waited exactly a minute, watching the sweep secondhand of his Rolex, Natalia standing beside him, her eyes trained on the street as he looked at her. Vladov, Lieutenant Daszrozinski and the others were hiding down the alley.

The door opened—Tom Maus, his good-natured, slightly gravelly sounding voice low, said, "You've been a busy man, Doctor Rourke—you and Major Tiemerovna have been very busy. Come in—"

"We have some friends with us. I wanted to tell you first."

"What kind of friends?"

"Two Soviet Special Forces officers and ten enlisted men, but they're on our side so to speak—"

Maus started to slam the door. Rourke stepped into it, pushing the door back. "Look—in a day, maybe six days at the most, nothing will be left. It's the end of the world, Maus—for real, the end of the world."

Rourke watched Maus's face in the grey-purple light, dark shadows blanketing part of it, but what light there was catching in Maus's eyes.

"You're joking—and it's in poor—"

"I'm not joking," Rourke told him quietly.

"He is telling the truth," Rourke heard Natalia whisper beside him. "I wish to God he were not—"

Rourke looked at her and smiled.

"What the heck is going on here?" Maus asked

"One last mission, to maybe save some of humanity. And we need your help."

Rourke watched Maus's face. The darkness was growing. Maus nodded, then. "All right, inside with you both—"

"Our twelve friends?"

"God knows why," Maus murmured, shaking his head. "This is stupid—but yeah—but don't mind it if some of my people keep their guns drawn—"

It was Natalia's voice. "Don't mind if some of my people keep their guns drawn, too."

Rourke made a single, long, low whistle, and as he started through the doorway after Natalia, he could faintly hear the shuffling sounds of twelve pairs of combat boots hitting pavement in a dead run.

Chapter Fifteen

Emily, the Polish American Resistance captain they had first met when landing in Illinois, sat at the far edge of the room, her ungainly six-inch barreled revolver on the table beside her. Vladov sat a few feet from her, perched on the edge of a heavy worktable. Emily's eyes constantly flickered toward him. A young man, very young looking, thin, a pleasant grin on his face, sat at the radio set, tuning the frequency. Maus had identified him—the young man working the radio—as his top field operative against the Russians despite the man's youth. A six-inch blue Colt Python was on the radio table beside him as he worked. And as he worked, he spoke. "We almost never use this radio—can't afford to. If the Russians picked up a transmission from around here, well, they'd know where to look."

"This is important, Mr. Stanonik," Natalia told him.

"Marty—everybody calls me Marty, Major—"

"I am Natalia."

"Natalia—right. Russian or not, you're awful pretty to be a major. Take Tommy there," and he jerked his thumb toward Maus. "Before The Night of The War he was in the Reserves—he's a major. And I'd sure as hell rather look at you, ma'am, than look at Tommy there."

"If this were still a gunshop and you still worked for me—"

"I know," Stanonik laughed. "You'd fire me—here—I've got it, I think," and he flicked a switch on the radio set in the storeroom near Maus's office. "This is Shooter calling Eagle Two—come in. Shooter calling Eagle Two—" There was no answer, only static over the speaker. "This is Shooter calling Eagle Two—do you read me—acknowledge. Over."

Static—then, "Eagle Two—code sequence verify. Over."

Marty Stanonik looked at his watch, then began flipping through a Rolodex file beside him—Rourke noticed it because it had been painted and was no longer black with a metallic framework. It was painted gold. "A gold Rolodex," Rourke said under his breath, shrugging it off. Stanonik was apparently reading off a series of cards in the file, "Series twenty zero eight—Tango—reading now. Bob, Jack, Willie, Mary Jane, Harold. Awaiting verification."

Rourke smiled to himself—the code was ingenious and simple. And the oddly painted gold Rolodex was its key. Series twenty zero eight translated to the time—eight twenty. Tango was the standard phonetic alphabet correspondent to the letter T—T was the twentieth letter in the alphabet and the first names Stanonik had read over the radio were from the T section of the gold Rolodex, apparently arranged randomly and read in a certain pre-arranged order.

The radio crackled with static. "Shooter, this is Eagle Two—verifying. Series twenty zero eight plus twenty-seven—" Twenty-seven would mean plus one since there were only twenty-six letters in the alphabet. "Uniform—repeat. Uniform. Mabel, Alice, Fred, Pablo, Maurice, Joe. Awaiting verification."

Stanonik flipped through the Rolodex—into the U section. Then he looked to his microphone. "Got a man here to talk with Eagle Two Leader—gotta make it quick. Shooter Over."

"Eagle Two is real busy, Shooter—give it to me—"

"Tell him it's John Rourke, Marty—and tell him to tell President Chambers I have confirmation of a worst case post holocaust scenario—six day countdown."

"A what?" Stanonik looked over his shoulder at Rourke.

Rourke started to speak, but Maus said it, "The man here tells me the world is going to end, Marty."

"Ohh, shit—"

Rourke thought the remark summed it up rather succinctly.

Chapter Sixteen

The radio was designed to automatically change frequencies and despite the fact that Soviet monitoring equipment existed which could still pick up such a set-up easily enough, it was a far better arrangement than a single frequency system.

"I cannot summon a large force, Dr. Rourke. But Varakov is right. I of course knew the post holocaust scenario possibilities and I was never certain the Eden Project got away in time before Kennedy Space Center was destroyed. I don't doubt that he has the data to support the scenario. I can send you a dozen volunteers. No others to be spared. KGB forces and Army units under KGB command have our backs to the wall here—boxing us in. Our only chance is volunteers from Texas. Reed here is telling me I'm stupid to be saying this en clare, but what's the difference now. We're going to fight. I should have known a set-up for a slaughter like this wasn't General Varakov's doing. They've been making strafing runs on hospitals, bombing civilian encampments—the whole thing. The largest troop commitment they've made since invading the continent. I've got a volunteer, your old friend Colonel Reed. Where do I send him and the man he'll take with him?"

Chambers' radio procedure left a great deal to be desired, Rourke thought. "I saw Reed with a western novel once. I recall reading the author was particularly interested in a certain location. For four reasons. See if he understands—Rourke over."

It was Reed's voice, half laughing. "Rourke—I'd love to meet you there—love it."

Rourke nodded unnecessarily to the voice so far away, then said, "As quick as you can and bring whatever you can carry. Rourke over."

"Reed — over."

Rourke handed the table microphone to Marty Stanonik whom he stood beside.

He walked away from the radio set as Marty closed the transmission.

"I do not understand," Natalia began, looking puzzled.

"The most famous western writer in history. I've got a lot of his books at the Retreat — you should read them. His name is French for love. The Four Corners — where Utah, Colorado, Arizona and New Mexico's state boundaries all meet. I read about his interest in the area some years back. Reed — I figured he'd know, too. Lucky for me he did. And lucky for me you didn't —"

"Why?"

"A Russian wasn't supposed to be able to understand it," and he winked at her.

Chapter Seventeen

Reed stood in the darkness on the steps of the church, looking out across the wooded area beyond the parking lot. "The men are ready, sir," Sergeant Dressler's voice came from behind him.

"Very good, Sergeant," and he turned and started through the open doorway, Dressler stepping aside to let him pass.

Military courtesy sometimes amused Reed, sometimes affronted him. Sergeant Dressler had seen active duty during the closing days of World War II as a tanker, served the country during the Korean conflict, been retired during the Viet Nam conflict and now — in his sixties — was once again in uniform. That a man of Dressler's age and experience should step aside for him — Reed — seemed somehow wrong.

But it was too late to change any of that, Reed thought, walking up the aisle toward the front of the church. "Ten-hut!" Dressler snapped.

Reed shook his head, "As you were — take your seats, gentlemen." Ten other men sat in the first pews on each side of the aisle. Reed stepped up the three low steps leading to the pulpit, just short of entering it. Reed stood beside it instead, feeling odd wearing a pistol on his hip. "All of you were told before volunteering that this was likely a suicide mission. Rourke couldn't get too specific on the radio — but I've talked with him often enough. Apparently the Russians have some move afoot to destroy what was called the Eden Project. Our earth — well, we told you that, too. In six days at the most, perhaps at dawn tomorrow, the sky will catch

57

fire, the atmosphere will all but completely burn away and the earth itself will burn. We'll all die then anyway. But apparently the Russians have some system for surviving it somewhere. My guess is the old Norad headquarters at Cheyenne Mountain but we won't know that until we rendezvous with Rourke and his force. It's our job to knock out the Russian base, so they can't survive the holocaust. Otherwise, when the 138 people of the Eden Project return to earth, the KGB'll be waiting for them, to shoot down the space shuttles before they land. And the Russians will have won it all, Communism will have the ultimate triumph. We owe it to the future, if there is one, and to every man and woman alive today or whoever lived, whoever sacrificed life or security or pleasure to defend the ideal of freedom — we owe it to all of them not to let Communism win, not to let the KGB be the masters of earth. And dying fighting for that is a hell of a lot better — " and he felt sorry for the word, remembering suddenly he stood in a church — "a lot better than being incinerated when the end comes. Are there any questions?"

A young face at the far end of the right hand pew — "What is it, Corporal?"

The man stood. "Sir, I mean, I know what you say is right, but what can twelve of us do — well — "

"Against the might of the Soviet Union? Well, not just twelve, Rourke has some volunteers — he didn't specify. Maybe a Resistance group or something. Say maybe there'll be a couple dozen of us. And what can we do? Everything. Anything. Die if that's the only way. But we'll do what we can, soldier — that's what we're here for, isn't it? I don't mean just here, in this church, at this briefing. I mean here on earth for. To do what we can. And now we have a chance unique in all of history. Sometimes people have accused me of being a little too far to the right, a little too anti-Communist. Maybe I was. Maybe I am. But we have a chance to rid the world of an evil, an evil that contemplates shooting the only survivors of the civilized world, of the democracies — shooting the only survivors out of the sky. I don't know how, again, Dr. Rourke couldn't be too specific. Maybe particle beam weapons like supposedly they used to zap some of our missiles on The Night of The War. But whatever it is, whatever it takes, I don't want a single man with me who isn't ready to give it his best shot. Maybe we've got the chance here to eradicate all the pent-up evil in the world all at once, to give mankind a fresh start five hundred years from now. And maybe we don't — but as Americans, well — we gotta try it." Reed cleared his throat. He looked at the Timex on his wrist. "We should be moving out. Any man who wants not to go, well, stay in the church here a while and pray for those of us who do. I won't think any the less of you."

"I think we all wanna go, sir," Sergeant Dressler said, standing. "But could you maybe lead us in a moment's prayer, sir?"

"I'd rather you would, Sergeant. I'm not too experienced at praying."

"Colonel, sir, I think the men'd rather that you did, sir."

Reed nodded, closing his eyes, bowing his head. "Heavenly Father — help us to see your will and to do it. And bless us all for trying. Amen."

He looked up. "Like I said, Sergeant — I'm an amateur at it."

"It sounded pretty good to me, Colonel."

Reed nodded, starting down the aisle of the church, hearing, feeling the men of his detachment fall in behind him. And then a voice — the young corporal who had questioned him. He began singing, "Onward Christian soldiers —"

The sergeant's voice joined him, "Marching as to war —"

Reed didn't know the words perfectly, and he felt almost silly — and his voice had always been bad. Before his wife had died during the bombing on The Night of The War, she had always joked with him that he couldn't carry a tune with both hands and a bucket. But he joined his men anyway.

". . . leads against the foe; Forward into battle, see his banners go."

Outside, the Sikorsky UH-60A Black Hawk Chopper was already waiting and Reed picked up his rifle.

Chapter Eighteen

They walked in darkness, Emily leading the way, Natalia
behind her, Vladov and the Soviet SF-ers after them,
Rourke, Tom Maus and Marty Stanonik bringing up the
rear. The airfield Varakov had arranged for the GRU pickup was still perhaps a quarter mile away, Emily, who knew
the countryside best, had told them. They had gone by
truck from Waukegan and into the farmland of northern
Illinois. They had been walking, Rourke judged, for nearly
a mile.

Marty spoke. "It's kinda hard to believe—I bought a
house before The Night of The War—I—"

Maus touched at the younger man's shoulder.

Then Maus said, "I've been thinking. Pretty hard about
this. I haven't mentioned it to Emily or any of the others
yet, but I'm planning on starting an all-out offensive against
the Russians in metropolitan Chicago."

"Go down fighting," Rourke commented.

"Something like that, but more than that. Ever since the
Russians moved in, they've been using Soldiers' Field Sta-
dium as an internment camp. Some other internment camps
here. They treat them well enough—that's where their
medical headquarters is at Soldiers' Field. But it's the idea,
the people there aren't free. Americans shouldn't die that
way if they have to die. Penned up, under guard. Maybe it is
that—go down fighting. They should have that chance, the
Americans the Communists are holding."

"I'll ask a favor," Rourke murmured in the darkness,
pushing aside a low hanging branch, holding it for Marty
and Tom Maus and then continuing on. "Don't make a di-

rect assault on Soviet Headquarters at the museum. Le
Varakov die his own way."

"Agreed," Maus answered. "That's the funny thing—th
way Major Tiemerovna spoke about her uncle, before an
in the truck just now, and what he's done now to fight th
KGB—General Varakov sounds like a good man."

"He is."

Marty said it, "Kind of stupid, isn't it—I mean, if you
assume we're good men, too. Why were we fighting each
other all these years?"

Rourke had no answer for him.

Chapter Nineteen

Sarah Rourke, barefoot, wearing a pair of the blue jeans her husband had stocked for her and one of her husband's shirts, listened to the sounds of her children over the muted sound of the waterfall to the rear of the Great Room. The children were playing poker with Paul Rubenstein and laughing because they were beating him at it, consistently.

He owed Michael thirteen trillion dollars, Michael had run to tell her.

Michael was a boy again. At least for now.

And Annie — there was a sparkle in her eyes and she giggled when Paul would tell her a joke. She had even blushed when Paul had told her she was a pretty little girl.

Sarah sipped at her drink, a book open on her lap — she hadn't begun to read it past the first line.

She had listened to music earlier — her husband's library housed records and cassettes ranging from The Beatles to Rachmaninoff, from original recordings of Enrico Caruso to Charles Aznavour.

The children had watched a movie on the videocassette recorder — she had been surprised that their interest had sustained in the original version of Lost Horizon starring Ronald Coleman. Perhaps it was the novelty of even seeing a television — the last program they had seen was the red haired Atlanta newsman warning of the impending Soviet attack.

They had played.

They had eaten the dinner she had prepared, not using the microwave, but slowly, lovingly prepared on the conventional electric stove. She had baked bread. She had made an apple pie using some of the dehydrated apples she had found in one of the freezers.

She felt human again.

Behind a series of vault doors in a cave inside a mountain in the middle of World War III, perhaps Soviet soldiers or brigands prowling nearby.

But she felt human again.

It was a feeling she did not want to lose.

But she could not concentrate. She worried that John Rourke still lived somewhere out there. That he would be able to come back to her.

And despite the fact the beautiful Russian woman was her rival, she worried—and she found herself smiling at the thought—for Natalia Tiemerovna.

"I'm crazy," she murmured, listening to her children laugh.

Chapter Twenty

The GRU aircraft — a Beechcraft Super King Air — had made its pass over the field, Vladov radioing to the aircraft, getting the proper recognition signal. There had been a schedule of appointed rendezvous times, five in all and this was the fourth.

The Polish American woman, Emily, who was a self-proclaimed hater of the Russians, had laughed as she had broken out the flares. She had said, "If I'd ever figured I'd be lighting a field so a bunch of Commies usin' a stolen American airplane could land safely I'd have had myself committed to the funny farm." But with Lieutenant Daszrozinski and several of his men helping her, she had done just that.

In the brush at the far edge of the field now, Rourke, Natalia, Vladov, Maus and Marty Stanonik waited, their assault rifles ready, the rest of Vladov's men sprinkled around the field with Daszrozinski and Emily at the far end.

"That GRU man is a good pilot," Rourke commented, watching as the Beechcraft touched down, bouncing across the field, slowing, slowing still more, then turning into a take-off position. "Makes me feel like a drug dealer waiting for a marijuana drop," he laughed, pushing himself to his feet, staying in a low crouch, running, the CAR-15 across his back, the M-16 in his hands, Natalia, Maus, Stanonik and Vladov in a wedge around him.

It was two hundred yards as he reckoned it — a healthy run with a heavy pack, several handguns and knives and two assault rifles. But he didn't slow or stop until he reached the aircraft, hearing Vladov on the small radio giving the code phrase, "Red, white and blue — red, white and blue —"

The irony didn't escape him.

The door in the fuselage opened, a tall, thin man appearing in the shadow and moonlight.

He looked down. "You are the American doctor?"

"I'm Rourke."

The man extended his right hand, hesitantly. Rourke shifted his assault rifle, holding it by the front handguard in his left hand, taking the GRU man's hand. "We had an expression here in America—I don't know if you ever heard it. Politics makes strange bedfellows. Anyway—I'm glad you made it."

The GRU man nodded.

Rourke felt Natalia's presence beside him. "I know you—you are Captain Gorki."

"Yes, Comrade Major—I met you once in Moscow—you remember faces well. I am Major Gorki now."

"It is good to see you, Comrade."

Rourke shrugged his shoulders.

Maus and Marty Stanonik, M-16s in their hands, were coming from the nose of the plane, dipping under the starboard wing. "You'd better get airborne and get the hell out of here," Maus announced.

"I was planning on it," Rourke nodded.

At the edge of his peripheral vision he saw Vladov and Daszrozinski, Daszrozinski leading the Soviet SF-ers toward the fuselage. Rourke stepped away to give them room.

The GRU pilot had hopped down, standing beside Maus now. "There are two of us—myself and a Sergeant Druszik. We will accompany you, Comrade Major Tiemerovna, and be ready to fly you out should that be possible."

Rourke watched as Natalia nodded. "We've got a slight change in plans," Rourke said, then. "I couldn't inform U.S. II of the exact rendezvous point we'd been given—the possibility of the KGB listening in. But I'll give you a new rendezvous spot—easy enough to get to."

"I have charts aboard the aircraft, Dr. Rourke. If you'll

66

follow me, while the gear is being secured."

Rourke nodded. He turned to Tom Maus. "Tom, good luck to you. I hope you can do what you plan."

Maus laughed, saying, "All I can do is try—don't have much to lose, do I?"

Rourke shrugged. He extended his hand to Marty Stanonik. "Pleasure to meet you, Marty. I wish you the same—good luck."

The young man nodded. "Yeah, knowin' Tommy here, we'll need it," and Maus laughed.

Emily was there as well. "Ma'am, without your help we wouldn't have made it this far. Thank you."

She said nothing, only nodded.

Natalia stepped forward, leaned toward Maus, kissing him on the cheek, then did the same to Marty. "Thank you both," she said softly. She turned to Emily. "And thank you, thank you very much, Mrs. Bronkiewicz."

The woman who hated the Russians, her voice barely audible, told Natalia, "God bless all of you," then turned and walked away.

Chapter Twenty-one

The Four Corners were not a precise location place wise, but geographically quite precise. There was a marker nearby Rourke knew — he hadn't bothered to read it, having read it years before.

He sat in the shelter of high rocks, overlooking the only logical landing site for an aircraft of sufficient size to land a dozen men and a crew. Natalia slept in his left arm, her head against his shoulder. Only Vladov, and two men, besides Rourke, were awake. Rourke had slept aboard the aircraft, as had Vladov and most of the men. Natalia had not been able to sleep and it had taken her some time after landing and coming into the rocks, their own aircraft camouflaged, until she had drifted off.

"The Comrade Major, she loves her uncle a great deal, I think," Vladov whispered.

Rourke nodded slowly, so some sudden movement would not awaken her.

"And she loves you, too, I think, also a great deal. It is written in her eyes. Women — even if a woman is a major in the KGB — they write their emotions across their eyes. For you, that is what is written there."

"I know," Rourke answered, trying nottural microbes, which had been all but ignored by commercial enterprises. The unexpected advent of recombinant-DNA techniques from Rourke. "What are they like?"

Rourke knew where the Soviet captain was looking — to his two sentries on the far side of the grassy plain which the rocks overlooked. "They're like you, like me, very much like us both, I'd imagine. So far as I know, only one of the men is a man I know personally."

"The Colonel Reed of whom you speak?"

"Yes, Colonel Reed."

"What is he like? I have heard of him before. The chief intelligence officer for United States II."

Rourke felt himself smile. "He is that. Strange guy — fluctuate from an occasionally bizarre sense of humor to a guy who wouldn't laugh if his life depended on it. He's a career man so to speak. Any Intelligence on active duty for a long time, then in the Reserves, then called up to active duty when all of this started — before the War."

"He hates Russians then." It was a statement Vladov made, not a question, shifting his position, moving the 5.45mm AKS-74 onto his lap from the ground beside him.

"Yeah, he hates Russians with a real passion."

"It is something very strange," Vladov said. "But before The Night of The Nar, I hated Americans very much. And I realized after our troops came in as part of the first invasion force I had never met an American. Not ever. I wondered how it could be that I could hate someone whom I had never come to know. I still wonder this."

"You'll turn into a pacifist if you're not careful," Rourke laughed softly.

"Yes, a pacifist. It would be most amusing for me to turn into a pacifist. I fought in Afghanistan. I served in a security contingent in Poland. It should be most amusing were I to become a pacifist, as you say."

Rourke chewed down on the end of his cigar — it was clamped between his teeth in the right corner of his mouth. There was no need to be particularly watchful, Vladov's men would do that. He closed his eyes. He said to Vladov, "I was pretty much the same way. I met Natalia, saved her life, and she saved mine — mine and my friend Paul Rubenstein's life —"

"This Rubenstein — it is Jewish, correct?"

"Yeah," Rourke nodded, electing not to mention that Na-

69

talia was also half Jewish as her uncle had revealed in his letter.

"In Russia, we do not like Jews—"

"You ever think maybe all of that was just as smart as not liking Americans?"

The Soviet Special Forces captain didn't answer for a moment, then from the sudden darkness when a cloud blocked the moon, Rourke heard his voice. "You do not hate the Russians?"

"I don't hate her, do I? And I can't see any reason to hate you. Do you hate me?"

"No, of course not, there is—"

"Reason?"

"Yes—no reason."

"Too bad," Rourke smiled. "Too bad we couldn't have all sat down like this before it all got blown up and destroyed, before this whole holocaust scenario came about—"

"Too bad, yes. This Eden Project—perhaps for them it will be different. If we can do what we have set out here to do."

"Perhaps," Rourke agreed. "But in a way, maybe it won't be."

"What do you mean?" Vladov asked, the flare of a match cupped in his hands making a rising and falling sound as the phosphorous burned, Rourke smelling the smoke of the cigarette mingled with the phosphorous.

"It'd be nice if somehow they could know what we're talking of here tonight, and learn from our mistakes. It'd be nice if they could."

"Yes."

"But I don't think they will—you got an extra cigarette? If I light a cigar, the smell'll wake up Natalia."

"I hope you like them," Rourke heard Vladov laugh. "They are American cigarettes."

"Any port in a storm." Vladov fired the cigarette from his own already lit one, passing it to Rourke. "Camel?"

70

"Yes, I like them. I used to buy them on the black market and smoke them in Russia, and in Poland, too."

"Don't tell Natalia I bummed a cigarette," Rourke smiled. "I'm always telling her to quit—that it's bad for her health," and he laughed, hearing Vladov laughing too.

"I had quit smoking cigarettes for two years, before The Night of The War. After this, I started again. It did not matter."

"Yes," Rourke told the Soviet captain. "It didn't matter." In the distance, Rourke heard the drone of aircraft engines. He turned his body to see his wrist beyond Natalia's shoulders, rolling back the cuff of the battered brown bomber jacket to read his watch. It was set still to Eastern time. In an hour or so, in the East, it would be sunrise. It was hard to think that in Europe, in what remained of Great Britain, perhaps the world had already ended.

John Rourke inhaled the cigarette smoke deeply into his lungs—wondering what it mattered.

But he felt Natalia's breath against his skin as she moved in his arm. And Rourke realized that it still did matter.

Chapter Twenty-two

Vladov had aroused his men, the men going out onto the prairie and lighting the flares already set there after their arrival. For the second time in the darkness that night, Rourke watched an aircraft land. But there were no radio communications — to have agreed on a frequency would have been risking the security compromised.

The aircraft — an old civilian aircraft Rourke couldn't immediately identify — slowed, turning, prepared for take-off, the fuselage door opening, men pouring from it, dropping flat in the high grass, the wind stiff now and the clouds moving briskly overhead, making the moonlight come and go with the nagging irregularity of a flickering strobe light, making the movements of Reed's men as they assumed defensive postures surrounding the aircraft look jerky, like something from a silent film that had been shown once too often.

Rourke had awakened Natalia. Vladov on one side of him, now, Natalia on the other side, Rourke walked across the prairie, the grass high, something he could feel as it moved against his Levis, the grass nearly to his knees in spots. Natalia squeezed his left hand in her right. He squeezed hers back.

He kept walking, toward the aircraft, seeing Reed now in a flicker of moonlight standing beside the wing stem.

He heard Reed's voice. "I should have figured you'd have her with you, Rourke."

Natalia answered. "I too looked forward to seeing you again, Colonel Reed."

"That's not Rubenstein unless he's grown a couple of

inches — got yourself a new sidekick, have you?"

Rourke answered him. "I found Sarah and the children. Paul was injured. He's recovering at the Retreat and looking after my family."

"Good for you — spend these last few days with them — why the hell are you here?"

"A job to do," Rourke answered, his voice low, stopping walking, standing two yards or so from Reed. He had seen the bristling of Reed's men when they had spotted Vladov's Soviet fatigue uniform.

"That's a clever disguise — he looks just like a Russian Special Forces captain."

"Colonel Reed, I am Captain Vladov, at your service, sir." Vladov saluted, Rourke watching from the corner of his right eye. Reed didn't move. Vladov held the salute.

"I'm not in full uniform, Captain," Reed nodded, gesturing to his hatless condition.

Vladov held the salute.

Reed snapped, "Shit," then returned the salute.

Rourke felt a smile etch across his lips. "Glad to see you haven't mellowed, Reed."

"You got any more Russians, or just these two?"

Natalia answered. "There are eleven other Soviet Special Forces personnel, surrounding the field." Rourke wanted to laugh — she couldn't pass it up. "One officer and ten enlisted personnel. In addition, one officer and one enlisted from GRU."

"Aww, that's fuckin' wonderful. What we got here, a Commie convention?"

"What we've got," Rourke answered for her, "is fourteen highly skilled men who value human decency over dialectics. You got any problems with that, climb back on your goddamn airplane and we'll knock out The Womb all by ourselves."

"The Womb?"

"One thousand of Rozhdestvenskiy's Elite KGB Corps,

one thousand Soviet women picked for their health and genetic backgrounds. Maybe a couple hundred support personnel. The president tell you about the cryogenic chambers?"

"Yeah, he told me."

"Well, that's where they're at. And particle beam weapons installations to destroy the Eden Project before they can land. The entire Soviet Politburo is either on its way to The Womb or already there. They'll all wake up in five hundred years or so—well. You know the rest."

"There are twelve of us—even. I'm the only officer. When do we get started?"

"I will order the camouflage removed from our aircraft," Vladov answered, taking off in a dead run.

Reed turned to a white-haired master sergeant beside him. "Dressler, send one of our guys—make it two of 'em—to give the Soviet captain a hand."

"Yes, sir, I'll sure do that," and Dressler started barking orders.

Rourke watched Reed. Natalia squeezed Rourke's hand tighter.

Chapter Twenty-three

Patches of snow dotted the rocks, drifts occasionally several feet high in the depressions as Rourke, at the head of the column of U.S. II and Soviet Forces, Natalia beside him, Vladov and Reed behind them, walked on. The two planes had dropped them what Rourke judged from map distance as ten miles from the main entrance of the Cheyenne Mountain underground complex. The light around them was grey as they walked, climbing slightly now, the Colorado Rockies air thinner, cold, and exertion telling on all of them, he realized, as he led them onward.

In another mile or so, he would send out an advance party to scout for Soviet patrols. But he waited, holding back. In a few moments they would reach the height of the lower elevation peak they traveled, and from there, be able to see the horizon.

If it were aflame, sending out an advance party would be pointless, for they would all be dead in minutes.

He felt Natalia's gloved right hand brush against his gloved left. "If it happens," he heard her whisper, "I shall love you after death as well."

He found her hand, holding it, climbing upward with her.

Thunder rumbled in the sky, so loud that at times it drowned the beat of his heart that he could hear in his ears. It was not the exertion, but instead what he knew might happen.

Rourke suddenly realized that if this morning were the morning, that his wife and his children, that Paul—if they had been caught outside, or failed to completely secure the Retreat—that they were dead.

If they had been inside, and the Retreat sealed, the fresh oxygen the plants under the grow lights generated from exhaled carbon dioxide would allow them to survive for perhaps several weeks until the air became too foul to breathe. The food would last for years. The electrical power from the underground stream—if the stream itself never reached the surface as he had always suspected was the case—would run on infinitely, or until the generators and the back-up generators malfunctioned and stopped.

But his family would be gone to him forever.

John Rourke loosed Natalia's hand, folding his left arm around her shoulders as they ascended the last rise.

The sun—lightning crackled round it in the air on the horizon, but there were no flames.

John Rourke put on his dark lensed sunglasses, staring eastward.

"There is another day, John."

"Yes," he told her, just holding her for a moment, watching it, for the first time in his life appreciating it.

One of the Americans standing behind them began to say the Lord's Prayer aloud.

Chapter Twenty-four

Colonel Nehemiah Rozhdestvenskiy stood beside the corpsman at the master radar control screen, watching. The blips — the corpsman had described them as an Aeroflot passenger jet and six Mikoyan/Gurevich MiG-27 fighters — were at the ninety-mile radius. The Aeroflot was a special craft, similar to the Presidential E4 747 Doomsday Plane which the late and last president of the United States, succeeded by Samuel Chambers and U.S.II — had not been able to use even to save his own life let alone direct a successful war effort.

The timing would be critical.

He turned to his aide, Major Revnik. "Major, order that the system be energized to ready status."

"Comrade Colonel Rozhdestvenskiy — are — "

"You have your orders," Rozhdestvenskiy nodded, not taking his eyes from the radar screen. Sixty-five miles now and closing. "Sergeant, order the airfield elevated for reception of the premier, the Politburo and the Committee Leadership."

He heard the sergeant who assisted the duty officer echoing the commands. "Duty Officer, begin tracking."

The captain nodded, answering, "Yes, Comrade Colonel."

Rozhedestvenskiy waited.

His aide announced, "Comrade Colonel. The system is energized to ready status."

"Very good," Rozhdestvenskiy nodded. He was letting them come in close. He wanted to see it when it happened, not just as radar blips disappearing from a screen. He turned his eyes to the high resolution television monitors overhead in the command center. They were faint, the images he saw on the screen at the center. "Greater resolution, technician!"

"Yes, Comrade Colonel," and then to another technician, "Bring up camera two—four, three, two, one—on camera two."

The image suddenly changed on the screen—enhanced, he realized. But he could see them.

One large, passenger-sized aircraft. Six smaller aircraft—the fighters.

"Excellent, excellent. Stay on them."

"Yes, Comrade Colonel."

Rozhdestvenskiy addressed the duty officer, "You have them."

"Tracking, Comrade Colonel."

"I shall take charge of the firing sequence. Do not hesitate to correct me, Captain, in the event that I should make an error."

"Yes, Comrade Colonel."

Rozhdestvenskiy picked up the microphone. "Firing center, act on my commands. Zero deviant flux on my signal. Ten. Nine. Eight." He watched the growing images of the six aircraft on the center screen. "Seven. Six. Five. Four." It was the ultimate act. "Three. Two. One. Activate laser charge through the particle chamber now!" He eyed the duplicate control panels in front of him. He had memorized the firing sequences, learned the very functioning of the system itself to be sure. He could trust it to no one else's hands. He served as commander and technician.

"Switch on. Charging—one-quarter, one-half, three-quarter power—full power. Boost two and three."

"Yes, Comrade Colonel, actuate firing," the technician's voice came back.

Rozhdestvenskiy focused on the computer readout diodes. "Boost ionization fifteen points," he called into the microphone.

"Boosting ionization fifteen points," the technician's voice came back.

"Capacitance function readout check," Rozhdestvenskiy called.

The technician's voice came back, "Ten to the fourteenth capacitance, to the fifteenth, to the sixteenth." The technician's voice paused for a moment. "Ten to the seventeenth capacitance—"

"Hold on ten to the seventeenth," Rozhdestvenskiy ordered.

"Holding on ten to the seventeenth capacitance, zero flux."

"Designating targets. Grid placement!"

Over the radar screen before him a grid of green lines appeared, masking the screen, Rozhdestvenskiy commanding, "Television—put up grid Theta."

"Putting up grid Theta on Camera Two—on my signal, Comrade Colonel. Five, four, three—ready animation—roll—two, one, punch up—grid Theta on Camera Two, Comrade Colonel."

"Very good," Rozhdestvenskiy murmured. The grid on the radar screen and the grid overlay on the television monitor were perfect matches. "Switching from radar to video on my mark," Rozhdestvenskiy announced. "Three, two—ready to switch—one—switch now!"

The weapons system was feeding from the video screen, the radar running now as a crosscheck—at the range visual more precise than radar. "Designating targets now! Grid fifteen, target one, twenty-six, twenty second delay, target two, grid thirty-eight, target three, grid forty-three, target four, grid fifty, target five, grid nineteen, target six. Grid twelve, target seven." He licked his lips. "Automatic target acquisition and destruction on my mark—six, five, four, three, two, one—Mark!"

He could see it on the monitor.

He had programmed the delay between target one and the taking of target two so there would be time for the camera to restore picture function, time for him to visually confirm the strike.

One instant — the Aeroflot aircraft carrying the Politburo, the premier, the leaders of the KGB — one instant it was there. A blinding flash of light, Rozhdestvenskiy involuntarily closing his eyes against it, counting from the flash. ". . . fourteen, fifteen, sixteen, seventeen." He opened his eyes — the airliner was gone. "eighteen, nineteen, twenty — " Another flash, the flash brighter now, the camera totally disfunctioning.

"We have lost our video, Comrade Colonel Rozhdestvenskiy."

Rozhdestvenskiy began to laugh. "We have lost our video — indeed — but we have gained something far greater. Tell me — to please stand by," and he laughed so loudly he realized all of them must have thought he had suddenly become insane.

But the master of an entire planet could afford the luxury.

Chapter Twenty-five

"Holy shit—what the hell was that—it's starting!" Reed stared skyward, Rourke looking upward as well. There was fire in the sky, a pencil-thin beam of light visible for an instant—Rourke shouted, "Look away!" He turned his own head away, the roar from above deafening now, Rourke sweeping Natalia into his arms, pulling her to the ground.

The roar gradually died.

Rourke opened his eyes, Natalia's blue eyes staring at him.

"Was that it?" Reed snarled. "But we're still alive—"

"That wasn't the ionization," Rourke rasped. "It was the particle beam system."

"But what is it that they were firing at to make such a loud—"

Rourke interrupted Vladov. "Those weren't drones. It wasn't a test."

Natalia, still in his arms, beside him on the ground. Her voice was low, even, steady. "My uncle had predicted Rozhdestvenskiy would do this thing. And he was right. He has just destroyed the entire Soviet government. He has killed them all. The premier. The Politburo. The heads of the various branches of the KGB. It must have been that for Rozhdestvenskiy to utilize the particle beam system."

Rourke pushed himself up to his elbows, the fire gone from the sky.

"All those people—he just murdered them," Reed whispered.

"Assassination—that's the better term," Rourke advised.

"I cannot believe this thing," Vladov murmured.

Natalia sat bolt upright from the ground, her blue eyes saucer wide as she spoke. "He has made himself—Colonel Rozhdestvenskiy has—he has made himself the master of the entire world should we fail. The total master. Rozhdestvenskiy alone."

It was one of the U.S. II troopers who spoke, one of the two black men of the group. "Me—ma'am—I don't like folks what thinks they're somebody else's master. We're gonna have to get that sucker. Get him good, we are."

Rourke got to his feet, helping Natalia to stand. Her hands were shaking as he took them in his. "The corporal said it, we're gonna have to get Rozhdestvenskiy—gonna have to get him good. Reed, you and Vladov pick some men—ones who can be good and quiet. Put out a recon element so we don't go walking into something."

"I'll take 'em, sir," Sergeant Dressler said, pulling his fatigue cap off, running his five pound ham-sized right hand through his hair then replacing the cap.

"All right, Sergeant, co-ordinate with Captain Vladov," Reed nodded.

"I think," Vladov said quietly, "that the good Colonel Rozhdestvenskiy has just made all of us into one unit, has he not?"

Reed nodded. "Agreed, Captain, for now at least," and Reed started forward.

Vladov just shook his head, turning to converse with Sergeant Dressler.

As Rourke started ahead, he held Natalia's right hand in his left—somehow that had become more important to him.

And her hand still shook.

Chapter Twenty-six

Rourke imagined himself in Rozdestvenskiy's shoes. He doubted the KGB commander had any more precise data on the exact time of terrestrial destruction than did anyone else. With his armored Bushnell 8x30s now, Rourke peered across the corridors of granite and toward the entrance of Cheyenne Mountain. A level plain was before it, surrounding this when Rourke had seen the complex once years ago—only from the outside—there had been a single twelve foot high chain link fence with electrified barbed wire at the top. Now, some distance forward of this, there was a second fence of identical seeming construction. He judged the distance between the fences as perhaps twenty yards.

Men armed with M-16s traveled the area between the fence in pairs, one of each pair restraining a guard dog on a leash, the dogs either Dobermans or German Shepherds.

The sentries were at three minute intervals, hardly enough time to cross the outer perimeter electrified fence and reach the inner fence, let alone cross it. Natalia had been given detailed information gathered by the GRU in her uncle's behalf, detailing as much as GRU had been able to ascertain pertaining to Womb defenses. Included in this information was the fact that in addition to the human and canine sentries, the area between the two fences was covered with closed circuit television cameras with at least four operators manning the camera monitors at all times.

Beyond the interior fence for a distance of twenty yards was a mine field, the exact nature of the mines something GRU had been unable to fathom. A smaller fence—perhaps eight feet high—formed the third and innermost boundary.

Running through the boundaries was one road, two lanes wide at best, which passed through the gates and toward the base of the mountain. Forming an outside perimeter some five yards or so before reaching the first twelve foot electrified fence were concrete barriers, these made of a special formula concrete of the type used to circle the White House following the attack on the U.S. Marine barracks in Lebanon, forming a shield against vehicles, explosives-laden or otherwise.

Rourke scanned along the roadway, toward the base of the mountain. Flanking the main entrance were a brace of 155mm M198 Howitzer guns—he imagined in the event something somehow penetrated the three fences, the concrete barrier and the mine field, not to mention the teams of armed sentries and their guard dogs. The doors themselves were fabricated of a special titanium alloy, given special heat treatment, constructed of various layers, the spacing between the layers of interlaced chain link and wire mesh. These were only the exterior bombproof doors. A short distance inside, a similar single door, twice the thickness, weighing literally tons, was positioned, this a massive vault door rigged to a combination lock system and automatically closing when the facility went to final alert status and unable to be opened until the alert status was cancelled in a specified manner. When this door was closed, automatically the climate control system for the complex would take over and the complex was hermetically sealed.

To Rourke's left—to the south—lay the airfield which served the mountain. A central section of the main runway functioned like the elevators aboard an aircraft carrier, able to raise or lower planes to or from the runway surface.

It would have been obvious to suppose, he realized, that here lay the chink in the armor. But a similar system of fences, guards and blast barriers formed a perimeter surrounding the field—although GRU doubted the area between the second and third (smaller) fence would be mined, this in the event of a landing or take-off difficulty. Teams of sentries utilizing guard dogs roamed the field in seemingly random patterns. As an aircraft would make an approach, the sentries would disperse, then claxons would sound again and the sentries would resume their random seeming patterns of movement across the field.

Once the elevator would lower an aircraft to the below ground hangar complex, there was a system of doors duplicating exactly the main door system. In addition, the runway elevator had sliding panels which could be brought into place to bombproof this opening as well.

Rourke swept his binoculars along the profile of the mountain. Spaced what appeared to be approximately a quarter mile apart were radar scanning devices, the dishes moving, searching, like hungry mouths wanting food.

At the height of the mountain, in what appeared almost a dish-shaped valley, but the dish of concrete, looking for all the world like a massive radio telescope, were the particle beam weapons. These were ringed by conventional radar controlled anti-aircraft guns and banks of surface to air missiles. The particle beam devices rose perhaps five hundred feet skyward on huge crane-like gantries. There were two of these and the mountings at their bases seemed mobile which would give each unit more than one hundred eighty degrees of movement and nearly a full one hundred eighty degrees of movement from the horizontal.

A low flying aircraft could get under their range of movement — but the surface to air missiles and anti-aircraft guns would take care of that possibility.

"I have been watching you," Natalia whispered from beside him. "Watching the set of your jaw, watching your mouth — it is impregnable, the Womb, isn't it?"

Rourke put down the Bushnell binoculars. He let out a long breath which became a sigh. They lay side by side in a hollow of rock which would keep them from overhead visibility. He said to her, "It's as impregnable as anything can be made. We can't sneak in, we can't shoot our way in, we can't blast our way in with explosives, we can't fly in, we can't rappel down into it. We can't even wait until nightfall—the infrared system the GRU said they have, the starlight systems. And anyway, the main doors are closed and the Womb is hermetically sealed in the event of the next dawn bringing the ionization effect. We can't even crash a plane into the particle beam weapons. A plane big enough to carry sufficient explosives wouldn't fly low enough to avoid the system, and even if the system were down and they didn't have time to bring it up to emit the pulse, the anti-aircraft guns and the surface to air missiles would knock us out. Maybe a thousand planes, all of the pilots kamikazes, each aircraft carrying a nuclear weapon—maybe that'd do some good."

"What if the particle beam weapons already had targets they were locked to—"

"The SAMs, the anti-aircraft guns again. And anyway, it takes only a few seconds to switch targets once the system is activated and charged—at least that's what your uncle's data tells us. And besides, even if we knocked out the particle beam weapons so Rozhdestvenskiy couldn't use them against the Eden Project when it returns, he'd have time to rebuild them, possibly once it was safe to move about on the surface again. If we don't destroy their cryogenics ability, a thousand highly trained men from the KGB Elite Corps would be more than a match for one hundred and thirty-eight men and women who are scientists, doctors, teachers, pilots, farmers—like that."

"Perhaps the Eden Project shuttles will land out of range of the particle beam system," Natalia offered.

"Just postpone the inevitable—and anyway, if you were the commander of the Eden Project and returned to an earth where everything had changed, been obliterated, what would you do?"

"Use my onboard systems to scan for power supplies,

power sources—in the hopes of finding something left of civilization."

"That's why they built the Womb here," Rourke told her, "and not somewhere else. They'll home right in on the Womb, like kids running home from school looking for a snack. And there's no way to warn them. And if we could warn them, what would they do? Where would they go? Somehow, we have to get inside. And we have to do the job today. There might not be a tomorrow. And we have to get in before nightfall. And if we have any hope of ever getting out with any of the cryogenic chambers and the serum, we have to be able to get out before nightfall, too, when the Womb is hermetically sealed—otherwise, we're trapped inside unless we can get to the control center and beat the information out of the master computer which is locked into the defense system."

"It is impossible," Natalia whispered, her eyes wide, staring—at what he didn't know.

Rourke felt a smile cross his lips. "But that's to our advantage. Making it impossible for us will force us to try something thoroughly desperate, something only people who were doomed and had no alternatives would try. And that's the sort of thing no system of security can be made to anticipate."

"Then we have a chance?"

"If there's one thing I believe in—besides you, besides Sarah and the children, besides Paul's friendship—I believe that as long as you never give up, you've always got a chance. So yeah—we have a chance." And Rourke shifted the binoculars back to his eyes, watching the entrance to the Womb. Just what exactly their chance might be—of that he wasn't certain.

Chapter Twenty-seven

There was a certain let-down. He had accomplished all. He sat quietly in his office, smoking a cigarette, studying his Colt Single Action Army revolver which lay on the desk beside him. He would never need to use it again. There were no more enemies to fight.

He — Nehemiah Rozhdestvenskiy — ruled the world.

It was the dream of Caesar, of Alexander, of Napoleon, of Hitler, perhaps of Stalin.

But he had achieved it.

Twenty years after the awakening, his population could easily have tripled. It was believed that the cryogenic process served to restore the body while it slept. If that were the case, perhaps, he thought, perhaps —

His father had lived to the age of seventy-three. His mother still survived, well into her eighties. His grandparents had been long lived as well.

Perhaps, through the cryogenic process, his life span might surpass theirs. Disease on the new earth would be virtually unknown, the same process which would destroy all sentient life destroying much of the world's disease producing organisms.

A world without infectious disease.

He smiled.

The Eden Project. "A Garden of Eden."

And he would be its master.

A barren garden at first, but the plants, the embryonic animals which were even now being cryogenically frozen under the aegis of Professor Zlovski.

Rozhdestvenskiy touched his fingertips to the desk top —

soon he would touch his fingertips to the earth and give it life again.

Because of his abilities and his ruthlessness — one was no good without the other, he had always known.

He stood up from his desk, walking across the office, to stare at himself in the mirror.

Nehemiah Rozhdestvenskiy saw the face of God and it was his own face.

Chapter Twenty-eight

They had followed the course of the roadway leading down from Cheyenne Mountain. It was patrolled by four wheel drive vehicles with one driver and two guards, each vehicle fitted with an RPK 7.62mm light machinegun, each of the LMGs fitted with a seventy-five round drum magazine.

Rourke, Natalia, Reed and Vladov watched the road from a quarter mile distant. "I agree with you, Rourke, with all these people who speak Russian like natives—"

"We are natives, Colonel," Vladov interjected.

Rourke laughed.

"Anyway," Reed observed, "we might be able to bluff our way through if we can take over one of the smaller convoys. But how the hell we're gonna do that with those patrols on the road I don't know."

"In the Chicago espionage school," Natalia began, taking a cigarette, Rourke lighting it for her with his Zippo, "we were taught that what is familiar is the least suspected. We can utilize this to our advantage. We have, after all, twelve men in Soviet uniform who are in fact Soviet soldiers."

Rourke reached out and touched her hand. Then he lit his own cigar, inhaling the smoke deep into his lungs, exhaling as he said, "I think what Natalia's getting at is that those guys in the road patrols can't be too high up the echelon. What if Captain Vladov and Lieutenant Daszrozinski just marched their men down onto the roadway and flagged down one of the patrol vehicles—then take out the guys running it."

"And then," Natalia smiled, "the captain could replace

the three soldiers with three of his own men. It would merely be a matter of changing uniform blouses. The vehicle proceeds down the highway toward a convoy of sufficiently small size which we had pre-selected. The vehicle stops the convoy. If another of the patrols comes by, it can be waved on. The suspicions of the convoy would not be aroused—there are so many of the road patrols that they must by now be a familiar sight to them."

"Maybe the Jeep could be given a flat tire or something and stopping the convoy would seem more natural."

"Exactly," Natalia told Reed. "And once the convoy is stopped, the rest of us sweep down to attack."

"We eliminate the personnel of the convoy," Vladov said, as if thinking out loud. "Assuming they are KGB, we take their uniforms—"

"Knives would be better than guns if we can get away with it," Rourke noted.

"Knife holes are more easily covered up," Natalia nodded. "And if the knifework is done properly, there can be little bleeding to stain the uniform."

"We get the convoy orders, drive up there and we fake it," Reed nodded.

"Maybe a little more precise than that," Rourke began. "Between Natalia, Captain Vladov and Lieutenant Daszrozinski, we should be able to get all the information from the convoy leadership that we need—and their orders—we can work on that after we make the switch and start back up the road. We won't have more than ten minutes or so until another convoy comes along. Vladov and Daszrozinski can do most of the talking—and we'll have to find the smallest waisted of the convoy personnel so we can get Natalia inside looking at least moderately convincing."

"I must dress as a man—I don't like that," she smiled.

"I like you better as a woman, too—but," and he laughed. Then he looked to Reed, "Why don't you send some of your guys down the road where it bends there to find a likely convoy—space men a half mile apart to use as relay runners to get the information back to us. We can't risk radio here. Don't know what frequency the convoys use, or what frequency the patrols use." He looked at Natalia. "You go with Reed's men—run the thing—" and he looked at Reed, "Unless you have some objections."

"I wanna get the job done—however we do it—I can object later, if there is a later."

"Agreed," Natalia nodded.

Rourke told her, "You pick the convoy—you'll have the best idea of how many uniforms we should be able to net out of how many vehicles. Start the runners, then get back around here. I'll be up in the rocks, riding herd on Vladov and Daszrozinski's men in case they bump into problems. One of your men," and he turned to Captain Vladov. "I saw him with a 7.62 SVD with a PSO-1 telescopic sight—have him leave that with me so I can long distance any trouble you might have if I need to. I left my SSG at the Retreat."

"Yes, of course, Doctor."

Rourke looked at Vladov, Reed, and Natalia in turn. "We all set then?"

Reed said to Vladov, "Good luck—I mean with nailing that patrol vehicle, Captain."

"Thank you, Colonel."

Natalia smiled.

Chapter Twenty-nine

Reed had stayed behind in the rocks with Rourke. Accompanying Natalia, leading the American force, was the veteran, white-haired Sergeant Dressler. They moved along a ridge line at a brisk, stiff-legged, wide-strided Commando walk, Natalia mildly amazed that Dressler seemed to show no fatigue. There was still some distance to go and she opened conversation with Dressler. "Tell me, Sergeant, what did you do as a civilian, between the period of the Viet Nam conflict and your being recalled to active duty."

Dressler, sounding barely out of breath, laughed good-naturedly. "Not much to tell, Major, really. Farmer. Worked my farm, helped my wife meddle in the children's lives, watched my grandchildren come into the world—that's what I did. Had a part-time job with the city we lived near, worked on vehicle maintenance. But all I ever been mostly is a soldier or a farmer. How about you, Major, did you do anything before you joined the KGB?"

"Interesting?" she laughed. "I studied at the Polytechnic. I suppose I am qualified as an engineer of sorts, in electronics. I studied ballet—I studied that a great deal."

"I never did see a ballet, ma'am, not a real one, anyways. One of my daughters took ballet some when she was little. Watched her dance in some of them recital things they'd have every year or so. I bet you was pretty as a ballerina, Major."

"Thank you, Sergeant," she smiled. "I enjoyed it—a great deal. And when I became involved in the martial arts, it was vastly easier for me because of my ballet training."

"Ma'am," Dressler began walking beside her now, "you

think we got a prayer of gettin' in there and doin' what we gotta do?"

She looked at him a moment, then nodded her head, brushing her hair back from her face with the back of her gloved left hand. "A prayer, Sergeant — I should think we have that at least."

She had loaned Vladov her silencer fitted stainless Walther PPK/S. Rourke waited with the 7.62mm SVD sniper weapon to back him up.

A prayer — it was likely all they had, she thought. And the thought of that amused her and at once frightened her.

Prayer was not something taught in the Chicago espionage school inside the Soviet Union.

But as she walked beside Sergeant Dressler, she tried to formulate one.

Chapter Thirty

Captain Vladov walked briskly along the trail leading down from the rocks, Lieutenant Daszrozinski beside him, the ten other men of the Special Forces unit walking two abreast. He had intentionally taken no security precautions — friendly forces in friendly territory needed no such precautions and to bring off the ruse, openness, innocence — these were necessary, more crucial than guile.

He raised his right hand, signalling a halt. "Order the men, Lieutenant, to charge their weapons but to leave the safety tumblers in the normal carrying mode. We do not wish a sharp-eyed soldier to see something amiss. And not a shot is to be fired without my order."

"Very good, Comrade Captain," Daszronzinski responded, then turned to the men. "You have heard your commander, charge your weapons, leave the safety tumblers in the standard carrying mode. No shot is to be discharged — none — unless on the specific order of Comrade Captain Vladov." There was the rattle of bolts being cycled, the shuffling of feet, a murmur of conversation from one man to another.

"Silence now," Vladov ordered.

He withdrew the Walther pistol loaned to him by Major Tiemerovna from beneath his tunic.

He edged the slide slightly rearward, re-checking that a round was chambered. He gave the longish, chunky silencer a firm twist, but the silencer was already locked firmly in place.

The safety on, he tried withdrawing the weapon from beneath his tunic several times until he could do it smoothly.

His first target would be the machinegunner at the back of the vehicle. If his men had not dispatched the driver and the second man by the time he had killed the machinegunner, he would turn the pistol on these other two.

None of his men had spoken of it, but he knew his men well enough to read what they thought — to kill their fellow soldiers was something no training, however rigorous, could have prepared them for.

It was not to be looked upon as combat — but as murder, he knew.

He turned to his men. "Your attention. I shall say this once and once only. The cause we serve is the cause of the people, because it is the cause of humanity. Alone, we represent the noble spirit of the Soviet People against a menace to all humankind which we ourselves have created. The ultimate expression of Communism has been and is to serve the worker, to break the chains of oppression. Working with our American allies this day, however uncomfortably, we shall be doing just that. Serving the cause of the People of the Soviet Union and oppressed people throughout the world. Colonel Rozhdestvenskiy and the KGB — they have ceased to be Communists. They are barbarians. They must be liquidated. As your captain, it is not something I enjoy to order you into battle against your fellow countrymen, but the cause we serve is just. We do not kill our comrades, we kill our enemies. And we had better be as efficient as possible in this for once we penetrate the Womb, we shall be outnumbered at least forty to one. If the women and support personnel have combat skills, then eighty to one. But we are Special Forces. We are the best. We have been trained to march in the vanguard or hold the barricade. We take with us the pride of our heritage, the faith of the Soviet People. Our personal honor."

He turned away. Along the road now he saw one of the four wheel drive patrols. And he checked getting the Walther from beneath his tunic one more time.

Chapter Thirty-one

In the rocks above, Rourke watched—he could see Vladov and his men. He could see the sentry vehicle. He charged the chamber of the Dragunov SVD's bolt, running one of the 7.62mm type 54 R rounds into the chamber, his hand wrapping back around the pistol grip through the skeletonized buttstock.

He settled himself, his legs wife spread, his breathing even, his right eye squinted through the dark lens of his sunglasses against the light, the scope—more than fourteen inches long—well back from the action and closer to his eye than he would have liked, despite the rubber eye cup. But he settled into it, into the unfamiliar rifle, the weapon in his hands rock steady.

"What the hell's the range of that thing?" Reed asked from behind him.

Without moving, Rourke murmured, "Maximum effective range is eight hundred meters with the specially selected ammo the gun's issued with. But I don't like a single trigger system on a sniper rifle. And I don't like a semi-automatic in a sniper rifle. And I've never fired a Dragunov before so I don't know what kind of quirks it might have. And if I do fire it, the scope's gonna go banging right into my eye and so my follow-up shot's gonna be slow and likely gonna be off. It uses the same rimmed cartridge they use in their PK GPMG and the RPK LMG—high pressure load. Any more questions?"

"No."

"Then shut up and let me concentrate," Rourke rasped, watching now as Vladov led his men down into the roadway. Soon, a runner should be coming back from Natalia that a convoy had been targeted.

Soon, Vladov would either flag down the approaching sentry vehicle or attempt to stop it on the fly. Rourke settled the scope on the machinegunner in the back of the four wheel drive vehicle. A quick shot would put him away and give Vladov's men a chance to stop the vehicle before getting gunned down.

He waited, suddenly remembering when it had all started — when he and Paul had taken cover in the rocks above the wreckage of the jet liner and he had used his own sniping rifle against the brigands who were systematically murdering the survivors of the crash.

How long ago had it been, he wondered, not consciously wanting to remember?

And then the vehicle began to slow, the face of the man with the machinegun something he could read through the Dragunov's PSO-1 sight. There was suspicion written all over it.

"Watch out," Rourke told Reed.

Chapter Thirty-two

Captain Vladov stood in the middle of the roadway, his right hand raised. He shouted, "Halt!"

The vehicle had already begun to slow, but even at the distance, he did not like the look in the eyes of the soldier manning the RPK light machinegun in the vehicle's rear.

He had no story to tell — military small talk for thirty seconds or so until he could get into position, then he would draw the gun and kill the machinegunner.

The vehicle ground to a halt, the brakes screeching slightly.

Vladov approached the vehicle, the man beside the driver moving his AKM slightly.

Vladov kept walking, his men behind him — he could hear their combat booted footfalls on the road surface. "I seek information. There was a convoy, just going up the road ten minutes or so ago —"

"Yes, Comrade Captain," the man with the AKM began. "I too have seen this convoy — nothing seemed to be irregular."

"My opinion," Vladov rasped, "exactly — what a pity, no?" The butt of the Walther PPK/S filled his right hand, the silencer hanging up on the inner seam of his tunic.

The driver was starting to move his hands on the wheel, the man from the front seat opening his mouth, raising his AKM.

Vladov's eyes shifted to the machinegunner — the weapon was swinging toward him, the bolt being worked.

The silencer — "Damnit!" He ripped the silencer clear of his clothing.

Vladov thrust the pistol forward and pumped the trigger, the safety off before he had repositioned the pistol in his belt the last time. One round—a neat hole where the right eyebrow of the machinegunner had been. A second round—the bridge of the nose ruptured blood.

He swung the silenced Walther to his right. Daszrozinski and Corporal Ravitski were on the man with the AKM, Daszrozinski ripping open the man's throat with a knife.

Ravitski was thrusting a bayonet into the soldier's abdomen. Three of Vladov's men were swarming over the hood of the vehicle toward the driver, but the vehicle was already in motion, moving.

Vladov fired the Walther once, then again and again, into the back of the driver's head and neck. The driver slumped forward.

Ravitski had the wheel, leaning across the already dead soldier with the AKM, his hands visibly groping for the emergency brake.

The vehicle stopped.

Vladov shot his cuff, looking at the face of his watch—eight minutes, perhaps less before the next patrol vehicle would be along.

"Quickly—their uniforms," and he dropped the safety on the Walther PPK/S American's slide and started toward the vehicle. "There is little time, Comrades."

Chapter Thirty-three

The runner had returned almost the same instant Vladov had shot the driver of the patrol vehicle, almost the same instant Rourke had begun a trigger squeeze on the Dragunov sniper rifle. But as the driver had slumped forward across the wheel, Rourke had eased the pressure, then set the safety to listen as the runner detailed to Reed the particulars of the convoy Natalia had selected. From the man's words, it seemed that the convoy would intersect the portion of the road where now Vladov's men replaced the KGB in under ten minutes.

Rourke looked at the runner. "You rest easy here for a couple of minutes. Join us down by the road unless the convoy's too close—if that's the case stay here until it's through—don't wanna tip our hands."

Rourke pushed himself up, snatching up his own rifles, slinging each cross body to opposite sides of his torso, then picking up the Dragunov. "What the hell's that, sir?" the enlisted man asked.

Rourke looked at him and smiled. "Ask the colonel later—he knows all about it now."

Holding the Dragunov in his right fist, Rourke started down from the rocks, the distance to the road approximately six hundred yards as he estimated it, but slow going because of the rocky, uneven terrain.

He glanced behind him once—Reed was coming, his M-16 in both fists at high port.

Rourke lost himself in thought as he ran. He would never understand Reed. It seemed as though gruffness and abrasiveness were a shield he used to cover whatever really lay inside him. He had observed the growing respect in Reed for Vladov and his men, noted the grudging quality of Reed's remark to Vladov — good luck.

Rourke jammed a deadfall pine, sidestepping a depression that was covered by some of the lingering mountain snow — but the snow was sagged downward at the center, betraying the depression beneath. He reached the trail — it would be easier going now, he thought.

He glanced behind him again, Reed was coming, and from the sniping position in the rocks above, the runner was starting down.

Below him on the roadway, three of Vladov's men were already boarding the sentry vehicle, three others of his men dragging the bodies of the dead to the side of the road toward the varied assortment of large sized fallen rocks. To his right on a track which would intersect the trail down from the higher rocks, he could see Natalia, running, behind her the remainder of the American force.

If he could set it up properly, Rourke realized, they would have a solid chance against the convoy, but after that once they reached Cheyenne Mountain and tried to bluff their way in, he didn't know. But it was the sort of thing one had to play a step at a time, he thought, saying it under his breath as he ran, "A step at a time."

Chapter Thirty-four

Two of the Americans and two of the Russians were sent back up into the rocks, with them were left the assault rifles, backpacks and other heavy gear of the remainder of the force.

Rourke, Natalia beside him, Reed, then Sergeant Dressler behind her, waited in the drop of the far side of the road from the high rocks where Rourke had waited earlier with the Dragunov. The next patrol had been waved past by Vladov, the Jeep's hood up, Vladov proclaiming a loose battery cable.

Vladov himself had assumed the driver's slot aboard the sentry vehicle, Corporal Ravitski and Lieutenant Daszrozinski with him, the lieutenant manning the RPK in the back of the vehicle.

Once again Natalia had her silenced stainless Walther, freshly loaded. None of the AKS-74s were silencer fitted, nor the M-16s. Putting a silencer to a .45 was something Rourke had always felt absurd and revolvers could only rarely be effectively silenced. For the rest of them, beyond Natalia's pistol, it was nothing but knives and hands.

In Rourke's right hand now, he held the Gerber MkII fighting knife, the spear point double edged blade given a quick touch up on the sharpening steel carried on the outside of the sheath.

Rourke still carried his hand guns, but had no intention of using them. A shot fired would blow the entire operation, because in the mountains as they were, sound could carry for great distances.

They waited, Rourke listening for the first rumbling

sounds of the convoy. Three trucks, U.S. Army deuce and a halves, and two motorcycle combinations, these Soviet M-2s, the sidecars fitted with RPK light machineguns with forty-round magazines only as best Natalia had been able to observe from above the road.

What the trucks carried or how many men beyond the two men visible to Natalia earlier in the truck cabs, there was no way of knowing.

They waited.

Rourke shifted position, tempted to tell Natalia to hang back, let him and the other men join the battle.

But it was a ridiculous thought and he dismissed it almost instantly. She would not — and he doubted he'd be able to cold cock her so easily a second time. And she fought better than most men fought to begin with. So she was more useful in battle than any of the others.

He said nothing.

But he looked into her eyes — she winked at him once.

He winked back.

They waited.

Then he heard it — the sound of a two and one-half ton truck's gearbox, the roar of an engine. Then the sound of one of the motorcycle combinations.

There was no need to signal to the remainder of Vladov's men who occupied positions in the rocks on the other side of the road. They would have heard it, too.

There was the sound — a sound of steel being drawn against leather — Sergeant Dressler with what Rourke recognized as a Randall Bowie.

There would be no sound of Natalia's Bali-Song being opened — she would open it when she needed it and not before. It was usually her way.

No one said, "Ready," — none of them was fully ready but they were as ready as possible. Knives against assault rifles and light machineguns.

Rourke pricked his ears, listening as Vladov shouted to

the convoy. "There is trouble along the roadway—we must see your papers."

There was the screech of brakes, the sounds of transmissions gearing down. Rourke didn't dare to raise his head above the lip of rock and peer across the roadway.

"We must see your papers—who commands this convoy?" Vladov's voice.

Another voice, the voice with a heavy Ukranian accent. "I command this convoy, Corporal—what is the meaning of this? These materials are consigned to the Womb Project."

I must check your papers, Comrade Major—I am sorry, but I have my orders—from Comrade Colonel Rozhdestvenskiy himself, Comrade Major."

"This is preposterous—what sort of trouble along the road?"

It was like a stage production, waiting in the wings for the cue line to enter—stage right and stage left, Vladov's men and some of Reed's men on stage left, Rourke and Natalia and the others below the level of the road on stage right.

Vladov had been fed the proper line.

"The trouble, Comrade Major—it is very grave. A group of Americans and renegade Russian soldiers have infiltrated the area and are preparing to attack one of the convoys in order to gain entrance to the Womb and sabotage the efforts of our leaders."

"This is criminal—these men—they must be stopped."

"No, Comrade Major—they must not be stopped. Not yet—"

"Yet"—Rourke jumped up from the rocks, rolling onto the road surface, to his feet now, the Gerber ahead of him like a wand—a wand of death.

Vladov was scrambling over the roof of the patrol vehicle, jumping, hurtling himself at the KGB officer.

There was a plopping sound from behind Rourke— Natalia's silenced Walther, he knew, the AKM armed man beside the KGB officer going down as he raised his assault rifle to fire.

Rourke dove the two yards distance to the man standing beside the nearest truck, Rourke's right arm arcing forward like a fast moving pendulum, the spear-point blade of the Gerber biting into the throat of the man, Rourke twisting the blade, shoving the body away to choke to death on blood, Rourke clambering up into the truck cab—the driver was pulling a pistol, a snubby Colt revolver. In that instant—Rourke guessed the man had taken it off some dead American—Rourke thrust forward with the knife, hacking literally across the man's throat, blood spurting from the sliced artery, the blood spraying across the interior front windshield, Rourke's left hand grabbing at the man's gunhand, his left hand finding the revolver, the web of flesh between thumb and first finger interposing between the hammer and the frame as the hammer fell.

"Asshole—gave me a blood blister!" Rourke snarled.

He freed the Colt of his hand—a Detective Special.

There would be a blood blister.

Pocketing the little blued .38 Special, Rourke shoved the body out on the driver's side to the road, rolling back, jumping down to the road on the passenger side, onto the back of a KGB man with an AKM. The man was a Lieutenant. Taking the man's face in his left hand, as Rourke dropped back, he wrenched the head back, slashing the Gerber from left to right across the exposed throat, then ramming it into the right kidney, putting the man down.

Natalia fired the PPK/S, the slide locking back, open as the man in front of her went down to the silenced shot.

She wheeled, raking the silencer across the face of another man, then switching the pistol into her left hand, the right hand moving back. Rourke saw it, knew it was coming, the right hand arcing forward, the click-click-click sound of the Bali-Song flashing open, then her right hand punched forward, the Bali-Song puncturing the adam's apple of the man whom a split second earlier she had hit with the pistol. He fell back, Natalia wheeling right, three men rushing her, Rourke diving toward them, snatching one man at the shoulder, bulldogging him down, imbedding the knife into the chest, twisting, withdrawing.

Natalia's Bali-Song was opening, closing, opening, closing, opening—it flashed forward, the second of the three men screaming, blood gushing from his throat where she'd opened the artery.

The third man was stepping into her, raising a pistol.

Rourke took a long step forward on his right foot, pivoting, his left leg snapping up and out, a double Tae Kwan Doe kick to the right side of the man's head, the man falling away, as he did, Natalia's knife flashing toward the man, slicing across the gunhand wrist, the pistol—a Makarov—clattering to the road surface along with the last two fingers of his hand.

Rourke stepped toward the man, his right foot snaking out, catching him at the base of the nose, breaking it, driving the bone up and through and into the brain.

Rourke stopped, turned—

Vladov stood there a few yards from him—Reed was beside him—both men's knives glinted red with blood in the sunlight.

The fighting had stopped.

The personnel of the convoy lay dead and dying.

"No casualties," Reed murmured. "Looks like anyway."

"Many casualties," Vladov corrected. "Too many, I think."

Rourke said nothing.

Chapter Thirty-five

The trucks were rolling, Vladov and Daszrozinski each manning one of the M-72 combinations and two of the Soviet SF-ers riding the sidecars respectively to man the RPK LMGs. Rourke drove the first truck, his Russian good enough, he knew, Natalia had confirmed, that if he avoided a protracted conversation he could convince the guards they would encounter at the checkpoints outside Cheyenne Mountain that he was indeed Russian. Beside him, Natalia. She was changing into the smallest of the Soviet enlisted men's uniforms they could find. "If I'd wanted a uniform, I could have brought my own uniform."

"Yeah. But the Russians don't use women for details like this—and besides, dressed like a woman you're too recognizable to the KGB."

"Maybe I should take my eyebrow pencil and paint on a mustache."

"Do you use eyebrow pencil—"

"Not very often," she laughed. "But a woman needs to have one just in case."

"You shouldn't have ridden in the front truck in the convoy."

"I didn't have any choice," she laughed. "I wanted to be with you—and besides, you're the only man here I'd undress in front of."

"I don't know if that's a compliment or not," he told her, looking at her for an instant. She had stripped away her jacket and her black jumpsuit and her boots—she looked bizarre, a silk one-piece undergarment that somewhere at the back of his mind he recalled was called a "teddy" or some other ridiculous sounding name and black boot socks. "That's a kinky outfit."

"Hmm—I saw you when you were changing into your uniform — boot socks don't go much better with jockey shorts."

Rourke laughed. "If we get out of this — we can get the cryogenic chambers we can steal and the serum — we can get it to the Retreat — maybe get Vladov and some of his men there and Reed and some of his men. We could accommodate more than the six of us. And you can get things ready — I can go after your uncle and Catherine and try and get them out —"

"No —"

Rourke looked at her as she pulled on her borrowed uniform pants. "Why don't you —"

"Because you'd be killed — it's as simple as that. There are three people I care for in the world. I've resigned myself to losing my uncle. But I won't risk losing either of the other two — yourself, Paul. If you go, Paul will go, too — you know that. When I looked at his wound I realized he'd be at full capacity in another few days — by the time we get back — if we get — when we get back, you won't be able to stop him. You might morally excuse punching a woman in the jaw for what you considered was her own good, but you couldn't morally excuse doing that to Paul. No, I love my uncle — he's the only real parent I ever had — but I won't let you die trying to bring him back. He's ready to die — he feels he's lived his life. I don't accept that, but I respect it. You'd never get him out alive. If we pull this off, if we destroy the Womb's capabilities to survive the holocaust, if we steal the chambers, steal the cryogenic serum we need and destroy the rest, if any of Rozhdestvenskiy's men survive, they won't rest until they hunt you down or the fire consumes them. You'd never reach Chicago, you'd never get out of the city if you did. I won't let you go — if I have to shoot your kneecaps to stop you, I won't let you leave me."

Rourke didn't know what to say to her.

Chapter Thirty-six

The concrete barricades were just ahead.

Vladov had read the orders, then given them to Natalia—the trucks carried plastique, C-4 explosives. Rourke watched Vladov through the windshield, aboard the right flanking M-72 motorcycle combination.

In the second truck, Lieutenant Daszrozinski was wearing the uniform of the dead KGB major. In the third truck, Corporal Ravitski wore the uniform of the slain lieutenant of the KGB. The Americans were hidden in the trucks, behind the cases of C-4—not a convenient place to be in the event of a gunfight, Rourke thought. C-4 was quite stable as an explosive, but there was always the chance—

Natalia beside him, in male drag, the uniform of a corporal, said, "What do you think?"

"About what?"

"Will we make it inside, I mean?"

Rourke shrugged. "Tell you one thing, keep your mouth shut beyond a yes or no, you've got girl all over your voice. And watch your eyes— squint or something. They see those they'll figure something's wrong."

"Why don't I just hide in the back of the truck," she said sarcastically. "These clothes are uncomfortable anyway."

"Because if there is a fight, you're better than anybody else."

"Except you, maybe."

"Maybe," said Rourke glanced at her and laughed. "My ego will be bruised."

"Your ego is too big to bruise," she laughed.

"Touche," he nodded.

There was another convoy in front of them and Rourke slowed the truck, then stopped, the two M-72 motorcycle combinations stopping as well. Already, in the sideview mirrors, he could see Daszrozinski and Ravitski climbing out — to do the impatient officer routine while the convoy was forced to wait. Rourke felt Natalia's left hand against his right thigh, groping for his hand — her palm sweated.

"That's another thing that'll blow your disguise," he murmured. "Holding my hand." And she started to take her hand away, but Rourke held it tight. "But I'll tell you when it gets dangerous and you have to stop."

Chapter Thirty-seven

"We've gotta assume that Lieutenant Feltcher never made it through to contact the TVM, so we're in this thing against the KGB and the Army units under their control all alone."

Sam Chambers studied the faces of his officers and his senior non-coms. He looked away from them, up into the barn rafters for a moment, trying to search for the right words. He turned his face back to his men. "I—I don't know what to say. I was never a politician—I was a scientist basically—I guess that was all I ever wanted to be. As your president, I should be able to say something consoling, something inspirational to you at this time. The Russians are closing in from both flanks, we have enough aircraft to evacuate some key personnel, but there isn't any point to it. A dawn today, I considered the fact that God had given us another day of life. By dawn tomorrow or the next day or within a few days after that, the world will be ending. As a scientist, I had no means at my disposal to confirm or deny any of the hypotheses formed for post-war scenarios. But the Supreme Soviet Commander, General Varakov, had access to scientific data. High altitude test flights were still available options to the Soviets, as a means of confirming the level of ionization and the rate of buildup. As a scientist, it might be a pat answer for me to say that I blame myself and other scientists for developing weapons systems and delivery systems which were capable of bringing about the destruction of our planet. Or I could shift the blame to the military for weapons build-ups. Or to the citizens of the various nuclear powers for letting their governments go on a headlong path to destruction.

"But the truth is," Chambers continued, "that I don't know who to blame. I blame myself as an individual matter of conscience. And maybe each of us should do that. And you can't say that the anti-nuclear people were right and somebody else was wrong. Because they never gave us an alternative to nuclear defense as a deterrent to warfare. But of course we never gave them an alternative to warfare as a way of solving problems. But I don't think we were put here—however we were put here—to lie down and die. And I don't think we were put here to compromise our beliefs and principles in order just to cling to life for a little while longer.

"So," he nodded, "God gave us this extra day. It's clear our Soviet adversaries don't know of the coming holocaust. I think it's up to us to use this day—in the defense of an ideal that somehow, even after all mankind is dead—somewhere there is a spark that won't die. I'm talking about liberty. That's all I have to say besides God bless us all."

It started with one man, then another and then still another—hands clapped to applause, but Samuel Chambers, first and last president of United States II, realized the applause were not for the words he had uttered, but for the feelings the words echoed from the hearts of the Americans he stood before.

Unashamed, as he stood there beneath the rafters, Sam Chambers wept.

Chapter Thirty-eight

The convoy ahead of them was moving up, the traffic officer near the concrete barricades waving them ahead. Rourke dutifully waited for Daszrozinski, disguised as the KGB major with the convoy, to gesture for him to move out. Rourke double clutched to get the old transmission into gear, easing up on the clutch, letting the truck barely more than idle forward, toward the barricades, the M-72 motorcycle combinations falling in at the front of the convoy, just ahead of Rourke—he could see a dark stain near the small of the back on the uniform Vladov wore—blood. He hoped no one else could see it. It wasn't the sort of spot one cut oneself shaving.

Natalia whispered, "Like they say in your American movies—dark of the moon."

"Yeah," Rourke nodded, letting out a long sigh, letting the vehicle roll ahead without feeding it much gas.

He knew where Natalia had her Bali-Song knife—inside the right front trouser pocket. Her hand rested over it. She had laughed when she had placed it there, saying that by moving the pocket lining to the side, with the knife there she might convince a casual observer she had something between her legs that really wasn't there.

Rourke hadn't found the remark amusing.

The M-72 combinations were flagged to a halt just past the sentry box, between the first and second fence.

Rourke braked the deuce and a half.

In the sideview mirror, he could see Daszrozinski walking up toward the head of the column, Ravitski, still disguised as a KGB lieutenant, walking beside him and slightly behind at his left side.

The guard sergeant from the sentry box snapped to and saluted Daszrozinski. Smartly, but not too smartly, Daszrozinski returned the salute. Through Natalia's open passenger side window, Rourke could hear as Daszrozinski and the guard sergeant spoke. "Comrade Major—your papers, please."

Daszrozinski was playing it to the hilt, removing one glove very casually yet very definitely, gesturing with a nod of the head to Ravitski to produce the papers.

Inside himself, Rourke waited for Ravitski to make some sort of mistake, show some sort of deference to the guard sergeant who in real life outranked him, Ravitski only a corporal.

But Ravitski, a studied air of surliness about him, handed the papers to the sergeant.

The sergeant saluted and moved off with the papers.

Daszrozinski lit a cigarette, offering one to Ravitski. Ravitski lit up as well.

Rourke eyed Natalia, shifting his focus from the two men just beyond her, outside the cab—she was licking her lips. He didn't know if in need of a cigarette herself or simply from nervousness.

Her hair was pulled back and up, stuffed under her garrison cap—the cheekbones would give her away, the set of the mouth.

Rourke shifted his gaze to Daszrozinski, the counterfeit major checking his watch anxiously.

He heard Daszrozinski telling Ravitski, "Give the men permission to smoke, Lieutenant."

"Very good, Comrade Major," Ravitski nodded, bowing slightly.

Ravitski approached the cab of the truck, leaning up toward Natalia, under his breath murmuring, "The lieutenant believes they are taking too long with the papers, I think—be alert, Comrade Major."

Natalia nodded almost imperceptibly, Ravitski concluding as he stepped down from the running board, "But watch how you extinguish your cigarettes—these are explosives we carry—remember," and he walked on toward the next truck.

Natalia took out a cigarette—Rourke slapped his hand against her left thigh hard, eyeing the cigarette case—one of the type that looked like a smaller version of a woman's handbag. Quickly, she took two cigarettes, putting the case under her tunic. She raised her eyebrows.

Rourke lit her cigarette, taking one and lighting it for himself—a Pall Mall. He put away the Zippo, tempted to laugh as he watched Natalia posturing to smoke a cigarette like a man did rather than a woman, intentionally trying to make her hand look less than graceful when she held it, keeping her right wrist stiff, holding the cigarette between her thumb and first finger rather than between the first and second finger as she usually did, fingers extended.

She started to pluck a piece of tobacco from her lower lip—Rourke slapped her against the thigh again and she nodded, moving her hand away.

Rourke turned his attention to Ravitski who had rejoined Daszrozinski.

They still waited the papers and the return of the guard sergeant.

Rourke glanced to his left. Guards were there, but not seeming to pay particular attention to him. Rourke had purposely selected a slightly over large uniform tunic—both Detonics Combat Master .45s were under it in the double Alessi shoulder rig. In the times before The Night of The War, in discussion of survival, often he had been asked why as his primary sidearms for survival use he had selected the Detonics rather than a larger pistol. His answer had always been that in a survival situation, the need for concealment shouldn't be entirely discounted. And no other pistol, as he had told them then and still believed now, could be so counted on for trouble free reliability, maintenance free utility, and the combination of compact size and big caliber. There were too many buttons on the uniform to reach the pistols as quickly as he would have liked, but it felt good to him having them there.

He looked past Natalia again, inhaling the cigarette smoke

deep into his lungs, wishing he had a cigar instead, but the image was too capitalistic for a supposed Soviet soldier.

Daszrozinski and Ravitski still waited, but from the sentry box now, Rourke saw the guard sergeant and an officer, a major, coming forward. Like the guard sergeant, the major was KGB.

Daszrozinski and the major from the sentry box exchanged curt salutes, Rourke overhearing as the new major informed Daszrozinski, "I am sorry for this regrettable delay, Comrade, but the experiments inside the Womb reach a critical stage now—in another week, security can be lessened I am sure and future shipments will be less delayed."

Rourke felt a smile cross his lips—the impending ionization effect, hence the real purpose of the Womb, were being held secret from those not part of the project. Would that there were a way of capitalize on this, Rourke thought. But he could see none.

Daszrozinski asked, "Then we are free to move ahead, Major?"

"You certainly are, Comrade—but because of the security restrictions, I'm afraid your shipment must only be taken beyond the primary doors to the receiving area. From there, Womb personnel will take over the vehicles. We have arranged a rest area in a tent near the airfield while your cargo is being unloaded. For the enlisted personnel there is some of this American concoction known as Cold-Aid—"

"Kool-Aid," Rourke corrected under his breath, smiling.

"And for the officers, vodka or hot coffee, whichever one might wish. You will find other convoy personnel there and the wait should not be that terribly long until your trucks are returned and you can move down the mountain again."

"Excellent, Major, then we shall proceed?"

"Yes, Comrade, very good," the KGB major nodded, again giving a curt salute, Daszrozinski returning it smartly. Daszrozinski turned toward Rourke, waving him forward, calling something Rourke didn't catch to Vladov and the other motorcycle driver. Their machines started. Rourke could hear the KGB major telling Daszrozinski, "Major, there is no need for your motorcycle escort to enter the facility—"

Daszrozinski—Rourke barely able to hear as he started the truck—turned abruptly to face the KGB major. "Major, my orders explicitly state I am to provide security for the cargo of explosives we carry, security until the cargo is transferred to the KGB personnel inside. I shall follow my orders, thank you, Comrade."

The KGB major nodded his head to the side, shrugging, waving the trucks and the two M-72 motorcycle combinations forward.

Rourke let up the clutch, Daszrozinski jumping to the running board on Natalia's side. Under his breath, the Soviet SF lieutenant rasped, "What is the American expression?"

"So far so good," Rourke whispered, letting the truck roll forward past the sentry box.

The M-72 combinations passed under the lintel of the bomb-proof doors, Rourke involuntarily ducking his head a little as the cab of the two and one-half ton truck passed under it after them.

Inside, beyond the doors, he could see a vast horseshoe shaped turn-around, at the far end loading docks and beside these, the vault door leading into the Womb itself. The vault door was open as it should be.

Rourke whispered to Natalia and Daszrozinski. "Watch Vladov, he'll have caught your conversation, Lieutenant, so I think he'll make the first play."

"Yes, Comrade Doctor—"

Rourke looked at him, Daszrozinski saying, "I am sor—"

"In what we're doing, we are comrades in the real sense of the word—no offense taken, Lieutenant."

Chapter Thirty-nine

There was not an AK type weapon to be seen—as if Kalashnikov had never lived—the KGB personnel all carried M-16s and those few personnel who carried side arms wore .45s, the "U.S." symbols on the flaps of the holsters bizarre, Rourke thought. Natalia, as Rourke drove the vehicle into the horseshoe, murmured, "According to my uncle, they have standardized here on American weapons totally for the logistics of supplying the Womb and in the event that at some future date any buried weapons and munitions caches which would have survived the holocaust untouched might be found."

"Interesting," Rourke noted. "So the AKMs outside are just for show, just like the dodge about experiments—lying to their own people—"

"Yes—yes, they are," she answered softly.

Ahead of him, a sergeant wearing white gloves and a white cap cover was directing traffic, Rourke following his lead, aiming the nose of the deuce and a half toward the loading dock area, breaking off from the main horseshoe of the driveway.

There were more military traffic cops, gesturing for Rourke to move the vehicle around into a slot from which he could back toward the dock itself for unloading. "Whatever Vladov's play is going to be, it's gonna have to be quick," Rourke murmured, cutting the wheel into a hard left, intentionally missing the maneuvering bay, the traffic director shouting up to him in the cab, Rourke making a rude gesture—they were of equal rank, then backing the truck slightly, hearing the vehicle behind him screech its brakes, then Rourke cutting the wheel slightly right, edging forward into the maneuvering bay. He was stalling for time—time for Vladov. "Be ready," Rourke rasped through his tight-clenched teeth.

He brought the truck to a halt, then started into reverse, fumbling the gear box, making the gears grind, stalling again for time. He started backing the vehicle toward the loading dock. Once the first of the boxes was moved, the Americans inside the truck would be spotted—and push would have come to shove.

He let the engine die, making a show of starting again, letting the engine die, half tempted to flood it, but worried that he might so overdo the incompetent driver routine as to raise suspicion. Instead, he let the engine catch, then eased the truck back toward the loading dock lip. The traffic director was cursing. Rourke grinned at him.

Vladov and the other motorcycle combination driver had parked at the farthest end of this section of loading dock, near to the vault door that led into the Womb.

Rourke said quickly, "Tell the convoy personnel to disembark the vehicles. When they holler at you for it, tell them the men are tired from the drive and you're going to rest them—you outrank everyone I've seen out here."

"All right, very good, Doctor," and as Rourke slammed the vehicle to an uneven halt, intentionally bumping into the loading dock—watching in the mirror as the loading dock personnel jumped back—Daszrozinski jumped down.

"Disembark the vehicles. Stay near your trucks," Daszrozinski shouted.

Rourke could hear Ravitski, from the running board of the second truck, echo the command as the truck pulled into its slot beside them.

The third truck was still in motion.

Rourke cut the engine, leaving the vehicle's transmission in reverse, leaving the emergency brake off. He started down from the driver's side as the third vehicle pulled into its slot.

He made a show of stretching, but not so much a show as to profile the guns under his tunic.

From the loading dock, he could hear a voice shouting, "Comrade Major, the men are not allowed to leave their trucks."

"Captain, these men are tired. They shall not damage your precious loading dock."

"But, Comrade Major—"

"Yes—it is Major—do not forget that, Captain."

The conversation ended, Rourke smiling. From the tone of Daszrozinski's voice, Rourke surmised the lieutenant had always wanted to talk to a senior officer that way and was making the most of the opportunity of pulling his spurious rank.

Rourke could see Natalia standing beside the front of the cab, at the right fender, trying to stand with her legs apart, her hands locked behind her—trying to look like a man. It wasn't working to anyone who looked closely, Rourke thought.

He glanced toward Vladov, following Vladov's gaze. A ramp led from the level of the horseshoe up toward the level of the door into the Womb. Vladov looked at him. Rourke nodded, he hoped imperceptibly.

The loading dock personnel were approaching the trucks now—it would be time.

Each of the personnel inside the trucks—mostly Americans—carried five pounds of the C-4, liberated from the packing crates, the rest of the C-4 in the three trucks wired to detonate—Natalia had seen to that quickly after the takeover. The battery from the commandeered patrol vehicle had been wired into the plastique in the center truck, the charges positioned to blow outward toward the flanking trucks and detonate the plastique there. The last man out would leave the wristwatch commandeered from one of the dead KGB men beside the battery—set for two minutes.

Rourke knitted his fingers together, bracing them against his abdomen, working open two of the uniform tunic buttons as he did—the Python was under his jacket as well, stuffed in his trouser band. It would be the first gun he could reach.

The loading dock personnel were starting to lift the tarp cover.

Rourke heard the roar of Vladov's motorcycle combo, Vladov shouting in Russian, then in English, "We attack!" The

RPK on the sidecar was already opening up, Vladov racing his machine toward the ramp and the vault door, Rourke reaching inside the deuce and a half's cab with his left hand, awkwardly, finding the ignition switch, starting the engine. Still in reverse, the emergency brake off, the truck lurched backward into the loading dock and the men starting to lift the tarp, Rourke's right hand finding the butt of the Metalifed and Mag-Na-Ported Python under his tunic, ripping the six-inch Colt .357 clear, his right index finger double actioning the revolver into the face of the traffic director who was already pulling his .45. Rourke fired again, killing a KGB guard as he raised his M-16, men pouring from the backs of the three trucks now, assault rifles — M-16s and AKS-74s — blazing into the dockworkers and the guards. Rourke pumped the Python's trigger once more, gunning down another of the military traffic cops, snatching up the M-16 from the guard he'd shot an instant earlier. The selector moved under his right thumb as he switched the Python into his left hand, opening up with the M-16 on full auto, three round bursts punching into targets of opportunity as he ran for the loading dock, jumped, rolled, on the dock now, the Python firing once, then once again, shearing the nose and left ear from the face of another of the guards.

Rourke was on his feet, emptying the last round from the Python into another of the military police, the man's body jackknifing, his .45 discharging into the loading dock surface near Rourke's feet.

The tunic open fully now, Rourke rammed the fired out Colt into his trouser band, snatching up a second M-16, forwarding the selector, opening fire — he had gambled twice the chambers would be loaded and they were.

An M-16 in each hand, he started to run, for the vault door, claxons sounding in the air around him, shouted commands, curses, the M-72 combination Vladov piloted through the vault door now, each side of the door littered with bodies cut down by the RPK light machinegun. The second M-72 was moving along the horseshoe, the RPK in the sidecar firing at anything that moved beyond the loading dock.

Rourke saw Natalia, an AKM in her tiny fists, the muzzle spitting bursts of fire, KGB guards falling before her as she raced along the ramp, up toward the vault door.

Daszrozinski held an M-16, firing it out in neat bursts, cutting down guards on both sides as he covered the dock area.

Reed, along with a half dozen Americans, was holding the center of the loading dock—they looked like a picture of Custer's last stand, Reed at their center, wingshooting a .45 from each hand, the men kneeling around him, firing their rifles. Where Reed had gotten the second .45, Rourke didn't know.

"Come on!" Rourke screamed the words. "The vault door! Hurry!"

And as Rourke turned, the vault door was beginning to close.

A jeep in the horseshoe—KGB guards firing from behind it, Rourke turned both M-16s toward them firing as he ran the width of the loading dock, jumping, both guns going dead in mid-air, throwing the guns away from his sides. He hit the road surface, going into a tuck roll, coming up on his knees, in both fists one of the twin Detonics stainless pistols, his thumbs jacking back the hammers, both .45s belching fire as he climbed to his feet, storming the Jeep.

One KGB guard dropped, beside the two Rourke had already killed with the M-16s, a second man down, his head exploding with a double impact of 185-grain JHPs, a third one—his M-16 was firing, Rourke hitting the road surface, rolling up, firing out both pistols, fists at maximum extension, emptying the twin .45s into the assault rifle firer's chest.

The body rocked back, then slumped against the Jeep.

Rourke was up, stabbing both pistols, slides still locked back, into the side pockets of his uniform, jumping into the Jeep.

He found the key, pushing a dead man from the seat, snatching away the man's M-16—how many rounds the thirty round magazine still contained he had no way of telling exactly, but from the weight as he slipped the Jeep's clutch, it felt like it was about half full.

He let the clutch all the way out, stomping the gas, stomping down the clutch again, upshifting, taking the ramp as he let out the clutch and floored the accelerator—the vault door was nearly closed now—Rourke wrenched the transmission into third, stomping the gas, bracing the pedal down with the butt of the M-16—it was half empty anyway—jumping clear as the Jeep hit the vault doorway, Rourke rolling to the loading dock surface, the screech of rubber, the sound of metal tearing, ripping—but as he looked up, the vault door had bitten into the Jeep, the Jeep partially crushed, but the vault door open three feet wide at least.

Rourke started to his feet. One of the KGB guards was lunging for him, Rourke's left foot snapping up and out, against the muzzle of the M-16, kicking it to Rourke's left, Rourke's right hand hammering forward, the middle knuckles finding the adam's apple, crushing the windpipe, blood gushing from the man's mouth through his clenched teeth, Rourke's fist snapping back, then forward, the middle knuckles impacting the base of the nose, driving the bone up and through the ethmoid bone and into the brain.

Rourke's left hand snatched the M-16, Rourke's right hand finding the little AG Russell Sting IA black chrome, Rourke hacking the sling free of the dead man's body with it as the body fell.

Rourke wheeled, the M-16 still not in a firing position, another KGB guard lunging toward him. Rourke underhanded the knife the six feet separating them into the center of the guard's chest.

The M-16 in his right fist now at the pistol grip, he eared back the bolt—this one hadn't been chamber loaded. He'd bet on that and won—and he fired, spraying out half the magazine into the KGB defenders on the loading dock.

Two of Reed's men were down, one dead and one wounded.

Rourke fired toward the KGB force assaulting their position, emptying the rest of the magazine, killing three more of the KGB guards.

He leaned down, retrieving his knife from the dead man, shouting to Reed as he wiped the blade clear of blood, "Get your men through the doorway—hurry!"

As he rammed fresh magazines into the Detonics pistols—all he had on him were two spares and he was using them now—he searched for Daszrozonski. "Lieutenant," Rourke shouted, seeing him leading a small force of the Soviet Special Forces troops—"The vault door—hurry!"

Rourke started to run, firing the Detonics pistols at targets of opportunity, seeing Natalia reach the vault door, watching as she clambered up and over the half crushed Jeep. He shouted to her over the rattle of assault rifle and pistol fire, "Natalia—blow the Jeep so the door will close—get ready—" Like himself, she carried on her five pounds of the C-4—it would be more than enough to vaporize the Jeep—she was good at blowing things up.

Rourke glanced at his watch, then he looked to the center of the three trucks. Corporal Ravitski was running from the back of it, shouting, "It is set—the charge is set!"

As Ravitski swung his AKS-74 toward the KGB, three of the guards opened up on him, Rourke seeing it as if in slow motion, Ravitski's body seemingly cut in half by the assault rifle fire, his left arm severed from his body, his face shot away.

Rourke's pistols were up—he fired both simultaneously—the left ear of one of the three guards, the back of the neck of another.

He swung both pistols as the last of the three KGB men wheeled toward him, the M-16 already starting to make fire. Rourke fired both pistols at once—both eyeballs in the KGB man's head seeming to explode, and then the whole head exploding.

Rourke wheeled toward the vault door—a half dozen of the KGB guards were charging Natalia behind the Jeep—Rourke emptied the one round left in each pistol, taking out two of the guards, the slides locked open.

He jammed the pistols into his uniform pockets, not bothering to close the slides, running, diving to the loading dock surface as gunfire rained toward him. He rolled—a dead KGB guard, an M-16 in his right hand—Rourke wrenched it free, wheeling on his knees, firing out the M-16 toward the remaining guards assaulting Natalia's position. He threw the rifle—empty—into the face of another man rushing him, took three steps and jumped to the Jeep, rolling across the deformed hood, falling to the floor beside Natalia. "Take my rifle—I've got to finish this," and Rourke snatched her M-16, Natalia sliding under the front of the jeep, murmuring, "I'm wiring the explosives into the engine—it should create a shrapnel wave effect outward—get as many of them as we can."

"Right," and Rourke shouldered her assault rifle, firing as another group of the KGB guards charged their position. He had to clear it for Reed, Daszrozinski and the others. Rourke glanced at his watch—less than a minute until the trucks blew.

Rourke fired out the magazine. "Gimme a spare—"

"I don't have any," she shouted from beneath the Jeep.

"Wonderful," Rourke snarled. A KGB man was coming over the Jeep—Rourke rammed the flash deflectored muzzle of the M-16 into his right eye, snatching the just dead man's M-16, firing point blank at a Soviet guard less than a yard away, severing the man's head from the body at the neck.

The M-16 belched fire again in his hands, the guards falling back.

"Where did you get the fresh magazine?" Natalia shouted up.

"A nice man happened along and loaned me his gun—you almost done?"

"Almost—"

"Get up here—I need someone else shooting at these guys—hurry it up!" Rourke burned out the magazine, pulling another from the dead man's utility belt, ramming it home, working the bolt release, firing again.

Then Natalia was up from under the Jeep, beside him. "All I have to do is touch this one wire to the positive terminal of the car battery—"

"How the hell you doin' that without blowing yourself up?"

"I haven't figured that out yet."

Rourke glanced at his watch—ten seconds maybe, Reed coming up at the left corner of his peripheral vision, others of the Americans and some of the Russians following him. "Where the hell is Vladov—"

"I haven't seen him since he got inside—I don't know—but I heard machinegun fire from deeper inside."

Why weren't their people attacking from their rear? Rourke wondered. Perhaps Vladov and his man.

Reed was over the top of the Jeep, a .45 in each hand, Daszrozinski and three of the Russian SF-ers and the GRU major and the GRU sergeant behind him, running the ramp. Rourke shouted, his throat aching with it, "Move it, Lieutenant! Move it!"

Daszrozinski was up, diving across the top of the Jeep, his men following him, doing the same, Rourke tucking back, wingshooting beyond them toward the KGB personnel.

The flash of light—Rourke turned his face away, shielding Natalia against him, the sound of the explosion momentarily deafening him despite the insulation of the vault walls around them, the shockwave slapping at Rourke, forcing him down, still clutching Natalia.

Rourke rolled on his back as the sound of the three explosions died, debris raining down just beyond the cracked open vault door. "I have an idea," Natalia shouted. Rourke could barely hear her. "I'll just shoot into the engine block—to hell with the battery wire."

"Everybody up—away from the door," Rourke shouted. "Now!"

"You heard the man—move," Sergeant Dressler ordered, even Reed to his feet, running, Daszrozinski firing an M-16 over the top of the Jeep as more of the KGB attacked.

Rourke dragged Natalia with him, running now. Ten yards— twenty—twenty-five— "We're far enough—give me a rifle," Natalia ordered.

Rourke tossed her his, Natalia swinging the M-16 to her shoulder, settling the muzzle for an instant, firing, then running, Rourke beside her, the force of the explosion hammering him down to his knees, Natalia beside him.

He looked back—the fireball was already dying—screams were barely audible from beyond the vault door—but the door was slowly closing, and then there was a loud clanging sound and the vault door leading outside the Womb was closed.

From the far side of the high ceilinged area of the natural rock cave in which they were, near the vault door at the far end, Rourke heard machinegun fire—it would be Vladov. "Let's go—otherwise we'll be trapped between the vault doors for good!" Rourke started to run, Natalia beside him.

Chapter Forty

MiG 27s were closing from the horizon line to the east, Chambers shouting to his driver, "Get this thing going faster!"

"Yes, Mr. President!" The Volkswagen's transmission rattled, the driver upshifting into fourth. Chambers thought of it for an instant. He was the president — no armored limousine, just a liberated Volkswagen Beetle that had to be more than twenty years old. And he was running in it for his life to get the half mile down the road beyond the lines of the U.S. II anti-aircraft batteries.

"Faster—"

"These things don't go that fast, Mr. President!"

"Shit," he snarled. The MiG 27s came fast enough — he had learned Soviet fighter aircraft well when participating in a strategic arms limitation session as a science advisor to the Secretary of Defense, years before his short elevation to the presidential cabinet, and before his assumption of the presidency by default.

The MiGs screamed through the air above, machinegun fire chewing chunks out of the road surface as the MiGs attacked the U.S. II defensive position. And Chambers realized it suddenly — driving in a Volkswagen down an otherwise deserted road toward U.S. II lines they would have had no way of knowing he was the president, no desire to waste a missile to destroy them.

The Volkswagen's windshield wipers were working furiously, but dirt still streaked the glass and the Volkswagen moved ahead — Chambers estimated the speed a little better than seventy miles per hour. Ahead of him, there were explosions, fireballs belching skyward, missile contrails moving from the air to the ground, more missile contrails moving from surface to air. One of the MiGs exploded, then another. At the rear of the U.S. II position, there was a huge explosion—perhaps they had hit an ammo or fuel dump.

"Get us there, son," Chambers snapped.

And where was Lieutenant Feltcher and the TVM? Had he ever reached the Texas Volunteer Militia at all?

Sam Chambers told himself not to expect a miracle—but he closed his eyes and prayed for one anyway, all the while hearing more explosions, more death.

Chapter Forty-one

"What is happening, Major Revnik?" Rozhdestvenskiy grabbed Revnik by his tunic, twisting him around. At a distance well beyond Revnik and a dozen armed guards there was gunfire—machineguns, assault rifles, occasional pistol shots, from the far end of the Womb near the interior bombproof vault doors.

"A group of men, and one woman, have entered the Womb. They have detonated explosives at the loading dock—many of our men are killed, Comrade Colonel."

"The men—who are they?"

"I do not know—some of them seemed Russian—some of them were dressed in American uniforms, Comrade Colonel."

"Comrade Major," a young corporal interrupted, snapping to attention, rising from his position behind the barricade of electric golf carts behind which Revnik and his men had taken up their positions.

"I cannot be bothered now," Revnik snapped.

Rozhdestvenskiy turned to face the corporal. "What is it?"

"Comrade Colonel Rozhdestvenskiy, I recognized the woman from my tour of duty in Chicago, Comrade Colonel. It was Comrade Major Tiemerovna."

"And the man," Rozhdestvenskiy snapped. "One of the men with her—it would be Rourke."

"The doctor whom you have sought, Comrade Colonel?" Revnik asked.

"CIA agent, doctor, weapons expert—survivalist—he is all these—and he is here!" And Rozhdestvenskiy hammered the heel of his balled right fist against the wall surface. "Re-vnik, get fifty of our best men, assemble them here. I shall take charge of dispatching this Rourke and the traitorous Major Tiemerovna myself."

He started back down the corridor, toward his office. He didn't allow himself to run. It would have looked as though he were panicking, as though he were afraid.

He walked into his outer office, his secretary looking up, smiling, "Comrade Colonel?"

He walked past her, into the inner office. On top of his desk were papers, files, maps, intelligence estimates — none of these would do him any good now. He unlocked the top right hand drawer.

He reached inside, his right fist closing around the butt of his revolver. "Damn you, Rourke!" he rasped.

Chapter Forty-two

Rourke had stuffed all his belongings into the Lowe Alpine systems pack, all except the scoped CAR-15. And one of the Soviet SF-ers had carried it through when escaping the truck in which he had hidden. The GRU sergeant had carried Natalia's gear. Rourke fished in the pack now, no time or inclination to change from the borrowed Soviet uniform, but instead needing the rest of his weapons related gear. The belt and flap holster for the Python, the ammo dumps in place, the big Gerber MkII strapped there. The Milt Sparks Six-Pack with its six additional Detonics magazines. The Metalifed Colt Government MkIV Series 70, the Thad Rybka small of the back holster with the two-inch Colt Lawman MkIII, the musette bag which carried extra magazines for the CAR-15 and M-16 and an identical bag carrying extra magazines for the Detonics pistols and for the Colt, these latter working in the Detonics pistols as well.

Rourke stripped away the Soviet uniform tunic.

He slung the musette bags cross body from his shoulders, using the wide belt from his Levis to secure the Rybka holster and the Sparks Six-Pack in position. He secured the gunbelt for the Python as well, finding one of the speed loaders in the musette bag with the pistol magazine. He rammed the Safariland loader against the rear face of the opened cylinder, the ejector star activating the release, the loader dumping into the cylinder—six 158-grain semi-jacketed soft points.

He holstered the Python. Natalia had stripped away her uniform tunic as well, ripping away the necktie from her shirt, opening her shirt collar. She positioned the Safariland double flap holsters on their belt around her waist, checking the twin L-Frame four inchers. She reholstered the Smith revolvers, securing the flaps. From her huge black canvas bag she took the Ken Null SMZ shoulder rig, slipping it on, securing it to her belt on the off gun side. From the floor beside her, she picked up the silencer fitted Walther. She twisted the silencer free of the muzzle. "No need for this now. We can safely assume they know we're here," and she dropped the silencer into her purse.

She slung the purse cross body under her right arm, then shifted it across her back.

Vladov's men who had changed into KGB uniforms stripped them away. Beneath them were their own Special Forces uniforms, not the fatigues they had worn earlier, but blue parade dress uniforms, medals in place.

Vladov affixed the dark blue beret to his head, at a rakish angle, Rourke noted. "We will likely all die, gentlemen, Major Tiemerovna. We will die if we must, but we shall carry the pride of our unit to our graves." Vladov picked up his AKS-74, then looked to his men. "Five of you—you, you, you there—you and you—take up positions on both sides of the RPK and behind it — you," and he pointed to the fifth man, "will back up the machinegunner. The RPK will be dismounted and you will serve as the ammo bearer." He turned to Rourke, Rourke realizing Reed was now standing beside him just inside the flange surrounding the interior vault door. "We are ready to proceed."

"Where?" Reed snapped.

Rourke answered him. "We've got two jobs—to knock out the particle beam weapons so they can't be repaired at all. We've got to locate the cryogenics laboratory and destroy the cryogenic serum, and if possible sabotage anything else along the way—life support systems for the Womb—anything like that."

"And you are to steal as many of the cryogenic chambers as possible—this is General Varakov's directive—to save yourself and the major and your family — and perhaps some of the men who fight with Colonel Reed."

"And the men who fight with you," Rourke corrected Vladov. "Them as well."

"What the hell do you mean?" It was Reed, and as if punctuating his remarks, small arms fire began to erupt from the far side of the vaulted stone hall beyond the interior bombproof vault door.

"They prepare to attack, Comrade Captain," Daszrozinski shouted from beside the M-72 combination where he supervised the temporary defense.

"Very good, Lieutenant," and Vladov turned to Reed. "It may be possible, Colonel, that some of your men or my men may find sanctuary at Doctor Rourke's mountain Retreat and survive the holocaust. But I suggest there is little time to argue. And I suggest that it is more likely the case none of us shall leave this place alive."

The gunfire was increasing in volume.

Reed nodded, "At least I agree with ya on that, Captain. Which way, Rourke?"

"Past their position, to the left — if General Varakov had his information right. A long corridor — it should be a shooting gallery."

"You're always so fuckin' pleasant," and Reed stomped away, raising his men.

Chapter Forty-three

Nehemiah Rozhdestvenskiy knew the target. Only one person could have set them against him. The person was Varakov. And the target was the cryogenics laboratory. The microphone in his left hand—the hand trembled slightly—he announced over the Womb's public address system. "Attention all personnel. This is Colonel Nehemiah Rozhdestvenskiy. The Womb is under siege from within. Approximately two dozen American saboteurs and Soviet traitors. They are armed with assault rifles and handguns and possibly with plastic explosives. They are dangerous. Their objective is to reach the cryogenics laboratory and to destroy our very chances of survival. They are to be stomped out like the vermin that they are. They would destroy our plans for world order in the future. They are our enemies. All personnel are to be armed—male and female personnel. Ninety rounds of ammunition per weapon. The arsenal rooms are then to be locked and secured and guarded, appropriate officers of the day will take charge. Hunt these traitors and saboteurs, hunt them down, kill them. But if at all possible, two of them are to be brought to me alive. The sole woman, Major Natalia Tiemerovna, the treacherous widow of our late spiritual leader Vladmir Karamatsov, a hero to us all, in whose memory we still serve. A man—American. He is tall, muscular appearing. He reportedly habitually carries two small, stainless steel finish .45 caliber pistols in a double shoulder holster. His name is Dr. John Rourke. He is a terrorist with the American Central Intelligence Agency. The person responsible for bringing one or both of these persons to me alive shall be awarded the highest honors and hold great responsibility and influence in the new order that shall be formed after the awakening. This is my word. I shall personally lead a search and destroy unit in pursuit of these enemies. Find them. Stop them. Kill them. Bring Dr. Rourke and Major Tiemerovna to me—alive."

Rozhdestvenskiy looked at his hand—it had stopped shaking.

He would win—he must.

Chapter Forty-four

The CAR-15 slung across his back, an M-16 in each hand, Rourke sidestepped past the flange of the interior bomb-proof vault door and broke into a dead run, opening fire toward the Soviet KGB position where the corridor began on the far side of the huge vaulted room. The distance to the KGB riflemen was approximately one hundred yards. Spraying both rifles toward them in three round bursts, Rourke skidded on his heels, Natalia and Vladov catching up to him, Reed already running ahead with his own contingent and some of the Russians.

Behind them, Daszrozinski and one other man huddled beside the slowly moving sidecar of the M-72 combination, the RPK light machinegun blazing toward the KGB position as well, Daszrozinski's AKS-74 assault rifle blazing. Rourke shoved Natalia ahead of him, running again—there was no cover. Ahead, one of the Americans went down—there was no sense stopping to check the body—the back of the head exploded with the hit. Natalia snatched up the dead man's M-16 as she ran past, a rifle in each hand now, too, firing.

Rourke glanced back. The driver of the motorcycle combination was down, slumped across the handlebars. Daszrozinski pushed the dead man—the chest peppered with bullet holes—from the bike saddle, swinging on, driving now. The RPK still fired, but the assault rifle fire from the KGB position was heavy.

Ahead, perhaps twenty-five yards still, was the farthest left corridor. The lead elements of Reed's men had reached it. An instant later there was covering fire from the corridor mouth.

Rourke had heard what Rozhdestvenskiy had said over the PA system — mentally he had corrected the KGB commander. He — Rourke — had been an employee of the CIA, but was no longer. And he knew Rozhdestvenskiy knew that, but it made good copy to his troops. Rourke ran on, the M-16 in his right hand fired out, still pumping the trigger of the assault rifle in his left hand as he ran.

It too ran dry. He left both rifles fall to his sides on their black webbed slings. His right hand moved to his trouser band — the Metalifed Colt Government Model. He jacked back the slide, stabbing it toward the KGB position, firing, knowing that at the range it was virtually useless.

The mouth of the corridor was now fifteen yards. He ran, Natalia only a few paces ahead of him — the one article of clothing she had changed was footgear — the uniform boots she had worn with her attempted disguise had been vastly too large for her and stuffed with rags and paper. But she moved fleet footedly now, changed to her own boots.

The M-16 in her left hand was shot out now, but the one in her right still spit fire.

Ten yards, Reed's men laying down a solid field of fire toward the KGB position, Rourke leaning into the run, his lungs burning with it, the .45 empty in his right fist.

Natalia reached the mouth of the corridor, Rourke skidding on his heels behind her — his borrowed uniform boots weren't the greatest fit either, he realized, his left heel aching. Rourke dropped to his knees, swinging the CAR-15 forward from behind his back, the Colt .45 stabbed into his trouser band, the slide stop downed. He telescoped the stock, pulling free the scope covers, stuffing them into his shirt pocket, putting the CAR-15 to his shoulder, firing. Semi-automatic only, with the Colt three power scope he picked his targets — a KGB lieutenant, a shot into the right side of the forehead; an enlisted man and a shot into the neck as he raised up to shoot; another enlisted man in the right forearm; another man — he couldn't tell the rank — in the mouth as it opened—it never closed.

Daszrozinski and the M-72 were coming, the running man beside the car—the ammo bearer—jumping to the side of the sidecar now, Daszrozinski picking up speed, the RPK still firing, the gunfire from the KGB position less and less.

But from behind Rourke now, near the far end of the corridor, there was gunfire. Rourke looked back—Vladov and his men had gone ahead and they were meeting resistance.

"Shit," Rourke snarled. Rourke turned to Reed. "Keep covering Daszrozinski, then catch up to Natalia and me. Keep a small force as rear guard to back us up when those guys behind the electric cars start for the corridor."

"Hey, who the hell made you the general?"

"You got a better idea?" Rourke smiled.

"Yeah, but I can't say it in front of Major Tiemerovna. Go on—we'll cover ya—and I'll take care of a rear guard—go on."

Rourke nodded, ramming fresh magazines into both of the M-16s, saving the CAR-15, pushing it back across his back beside his pack. An M-16 in both hands now, rasping to Natalia, "Come on," he started to run again, the length of the corridor. Ahead, Vladov's men weren't falling back, but they were under heavy fire.

It was what he had said it would be—a shooting gallery, Rourke thought.

Chapter Forty-five

Pockets of KGB personnel were everywhere in the space beyond the end of the corridor. Mezzanines, ranked like vineyard steps, terraced, were ranked one slightly above and rearward of the other at the far side of a vaulted assembly area, office doors to the right, large metal doors, like garage doors to the left.

Rourke estimated the number of guns trained on them and firing as over a hundred and growing.

He flattened himself against the corridor wall, the RPK firing toward the tiered mezzanines, but Rourke realizing it would have little effect—the enemy numbers were just too high.

"Vladov, have your men strip out the five pounds of C-4 each of them has. Who's got the Dragunov?" And he looked around. The GRU major carried it slung behind his right shoulder. "Pick your best shooter, give him this. Have the rest of your men break up their plastique bundles into five equal increments, then have 'em mold them into a ball—as quickly as possible."

"What are you—" Natalia began, then her eyes lit, their blueness still something Rourke lost himself in as he watched her. "We throw the plastique like grenades, then we shoot into the plastique."

"You got it," Rourke nodded. "You use an M-16, I'll use my CAR-15, and one of Vladov's men on the Dragunov. Three guys throw, the rest keep us covered and them covered." Rourke turned to the Russian SF-ers. "Okay, how many of you guys have heard of the game baseball?"

Natalia laughed . . .

Reed had joined them. The pitching roster included three Russians and four Americans now, the rest of the Americans and some of the Russians in the rear guard unit — and already the KGB personnel from the earlier fight were closing on the mouth of the corridor behind them.

"Once things start to blow," Rourke cautioned, "we head for that nearest garage door — the major here," and Rourke gestured to Natalia, "and Captain Vladov will use some of the C-4 to can opener the door for us. Should be more of those electric cars inside — golf carts. That's all they are. In an enclosed space like this you can't use more than say a half dozen internal combustion vehicles and those have to be strictly controlled for pollutants and lead emissions. Maybe we'll luck out and there'll be a regular vehicle or two inside. Whatever, we get a vehicle, we can outdistance these people for a while before they get so organized that we can't reach the cryogenics lab at all."

"That'll be guarded by now, so heavily we'll need an army to get in," Dressler groused.

"Well, fine, I'll worry about that when we get there. And besides, Sergeant," and Rourke looked at the white-haired man, "we are an army, remember?"

Dressler nodded, laughing. "All right, you men, I want those plastique charges ready on the double."

They were being piled up like a stack of cannon balls at a monument, out of reach from all but the most bizarre ricochets from the terraced mezzanines. Rourke had freshly reloaded the magazine for the CAR-15 while they'd talked from the boxes of loose 5.56mm ammo in his pack. He rammed the fully loaded thirty round stick up the well now. Ready.

Natalia, prone on the floor, legs spread wide, the butt of an M-16 snugged to her shoulder called, "Ready to fire."

Lieutenant Daszrozinski — Vladov had selected him as the best man to use the Dragunov — was by the other side of the corridor, prone as well. "I am ready also."

Rourke positioned himself behind Natalia, standing, leaning his body into the wall for added support. "Ready—Vladov—call the shots."

"Yes, Doctor," and Vladov addressed the pitchers. "Gentlemen, take your first one pound balls—we will fire in volleys. On my signal." Vladov addressed the men providing covering fire. "At the count of three, provide the suppressive fire. One—two—three!"

Gunfire, the roar of it deafening, Rourke feeling it as hot brass pelted against the exposed flesh of his neck, his face, his forearms. Then Vladov's voice, "Pitchers—ready—prepare to throw—throw!"

Rourke saw the first grey blur, arcing high toward one of the upper level mezzanines, Rourke settling the Colt scope's reticle, snapping the trigger—it was shotgunning, not rifling, he realized.

There was an explosion, then another and another.

Two more balls of the plastique, Rourke hitting a second, another explosion, then one of the balls landing near the base of the lower mezzanine. There was a burst of full auto fire from in front of him, the ball of plastique exploding, chunks of the mezzanine structures were collapsing now, fires burning, glass shattered on the floor everywhere.

Vladov shouted, "Cease fire."

The mezzanines were for upper level corridors—each corridor, Rourke realized, teeming with more of the KGB personnel. "Aim for the mezzanines themselves—we make 'em so they can't be crossed, we can slow 'em down," Rourke shouted.

Vladov's voice. "There you have it, gentlemen, we must do better. Pitchers ready. Marksmen, we are ready."

"Ready," Rourke called.

"Ready," Daszrozinski snapped.

"Ready," Natalia answered.

"Suppressive fire—on three. One—two—three!"

Again the roar of automatic weapons fire, the hot brass flying, Rourke settling himself, a deeper breath, letting part of it out, holding the rest. A blur of grey, toward the upper level mezzanine, "Mine," Rourke shouted, settling the scope's reticle, firing, the explosion making a fireball in mid-air, part of the upper level mezzanine outwall blown away.

Another blur and another, Daszrozinski's Dragunov firing, then Natalia's M-16. Two more, Rourke firing, Daszrozinski shouting, "I have the one on the left!" Rourke and Daszrozinski fired simultaneously, both balls of plastique exploding in mid-air, the upper level mezzanines shuddering, a section of floor in the top mezzanine collapsing, crashing downward to the floor, screams, shouts of panic from the Soviets occupying the positions below. "We did it," Daszrozinski shouted. "We did it!"

"Make for the garage doors now," Rourke shouted. "Vladov, Natalia, run for it."

He glanced to the pitchers. "Guys, throw 'em hard right and fast — Daszrozinski and I'll get 'em — Lieutenant — let's go for it!" Rourke shouted.

"Yes, Doctor Rourke!"

Rourke settled the CAR-15, waiting, the first grey blur — he fired — another and another, Rourke and Daszrozinski's weapons firing continuously, semi-automatic only, most of the balls exploding in mid-air. More gunfire from beside him — the men who had been providing suppressive fire were potshotting the plastique balls Rourke and Daszrozinski had missed, chunks of flooring rising up, collapsing downward, screams, the gunfire from the KGB positions sporadic now. Rourke shifted his right eye from the scope, squinting it closed, opening it, searching for Natalia and Vladov. They were beside the garage door nearest, planting charges, one on each side. Rourke shouted to the men beside him, "Keep pourin' in the lead — we gotta cover Natalia and the captain — hustle!"

Rourke let the CAR-15 drop to his side, swinging forward one of the M-16s — on full auto, he made it spit death.

Chapter Forty-six

Reed and Sergeant Dressler had planted plastique charges—five pounds apiece—to each side of the corridor wall, the rear guard called in, joining the others as they ran for the garage door, no fire coming from the mezzanines now, only gunfire from the mouth of the corridor where a large KGB force—Daszrozinski had recognized Rozhdestvenskiy leading them—was starting an attack. Rourke hustled the others ahead of him, staying behind at the end of the corridor, getting as far back from it as he could, gunfire hammering toward him now as the KGB assault force ran the length of the corridor, at least fifty of them to the best he could count.

Twenty-five yards from the end of the corridor, Rourke swung his M-16 forward, spraying it laterally from left to right, cutting a swatch across the corridor, hitting first the charge to his left, then the charge to his right, then letting the gun fall to his side, running, a fireball belching from the corridor toward him—but it would belch toward the mouth of the corridor as well, and likely make the corridor impassable. He ran on, two more explosions now from ahead, smaller ones, both sides of the garage door buckling.

The smoke cleared as Rourke reached the door. Already, Reed, Vladov, and men from both the U.S. and Soviet contingents were working to raise the door.

Rourke threw his left shoulder to it, heaving, the door starting up, Natalia beside him, pushing against the garage door—it was up. And inside were a half dozen golf carts, connected to charging units. And, a Ford pickup truck, olive drab in color. And a solitary motorcycle. There were other cycles, but these really motorized scooters. But only one cycle. Rourke liked Harleys, but some of the Japanese bikes were very good. And the one real motorcycle inside the garage was a fire engine red Kawasaki Ninja.

"All right," Rourke whispered. "All right!"

He looked behind them. The corridor was still in flames.

He looked back to the bike. It was a racing machine — fast, responsive, perhaps one of the KGB officers had 'liberated it' from some showroom or some garage. Perhaps it belonged to Rozhdestvenskiy himself.

If the latter were the case, so much the better.

He looked to Reed and Vladov. "Gentlemen, like they say, start your engines. Let's get all these electric carts rolling. We can use them to block off corridors with the help of a little plastique. The truck — that can haul the bulk of us. I'll take the bike."

"Just like horsemounted cavalry," Natalia murmured.

Rourke looked at her. "You've got it."

He approached the fire engine red Ninja, the Kawasaki GPz900R, water cooled with transverse four-cylinder engine would redline in top gear at 145 mph or better. It was capable of doing a quarter mile from a standing start in under twelve seconds reaching speeds in excess of 120 mph.

For outdistancing the electric carts, he judged it would be adequate.

"Should we sabotage the other garages. Perhaps there are more trucks there?" Rourke looked to Vladov.

"I'm sorry—"

"I asked—"

"Ohh — no. No time. Just put charges on the doors and blow the opening mechanisms — that'll slow them down. Let's get the hell out of here."

"Rourke, what the hell you plannin' on doin' with that bike?"

Rourke looked at Reed. "Riding it, soon as I hotwire it so she'll run." There was the roar of an engine and Rouke

146

oked around. Natalia, a smudge of oil on her right cheek, ent up from under the hood of the Ford pickup. Rourke arted to work on the GPz900R Ninja.

But on a hunch, after a second, he felt along under the ring — his right hand stopped. One of the little magnetized oxes. He opened it. "The key," Rourke said to himself.

He shifted off his pack, tossing it into the rear bed of the ckup. "Natalia, you drive the truck. I'll stay right with ou."

Rourke handed her the CAR-15 and one of the M-16s and e placed them into the truck.

For safety sake, he removed the Colt's magazine, jacking t the round chambered in the .45 and replacing the round the magazine, then reinserting the magazine up the well. e snapped the trigger, letting the hammer fall over the npty chamber, returning the pistol to his waistband.

He mounted the Ninja, bringing the bright red bike's en-ne to life, the machine vibrating between his legs, throb-ng, ready to spring ahead. Reed's men were operating the ectric golf carts, Vladov's men riding shotgun with them, eed and Vladov in the truck bed with the rest of the men.

"Ready?"

"I placed the charges," Vladov nodded. "Daszrozinski d I."

Rourke nodded. "Let's get the hell out of here," and very owly he let the Ninja out.

Chapter Forty-seven

Revnik turned to look at Rozhdestvenskiy. "They ha‸ sabotaged all of the garage doors, Comrade Colonel, six ‹ our men were killed in attempting to open them — trip wir and—"

Rozhdestvenskiy snarled, "Shut up, Major. The conten‸ of the third garage—"

"Nothing was harmed, Comrade Colonel, but the door destroyed and blocks the—"

"Have the door removed. The assault vans, my car, t‸ motorcycles—I want them out of there—now. Not fi‸ minutes from now—now!"

Rozhdestvenskiy turned and walked toward the first g‸ rage. The Ford pickup truck which had been inside wou‸ be of little consequence. He doubted with all of the poll‸ tion control equipment it was capable of any great spee‸ The electric cars—golf carts—would have been taken ‸ form corridor barricades as Rourke, Major Tiemerov‸ and the others fought their way toward the cryogenics lab‸ ratory at the heart of the Womb. If they took the most dire‸ route, they would have four miles to travel. An indire‸ route would consume as many as twenty miles, the passag‸ winding as they did from one level to another.

But the motorcycle was very fast. There had been ‸ room for it in the third garage where his car was kept and ‸ he had left it in the first garage. He mentally scourged hir‸ self for the laxness.

All about him was rubble, the terraced mezzanines whi‸ formed connecting bridges from one side of the mounta‸ to the other in this section of the Womb complex were d‸

stroyed. More than one hundred and fifty of his men were dead or critically injured.

Their goals would be twofold — to destroy the cryogenics equipment, perhaps to steal some of it for themselves. And to destroy the particle beam weapons atop the mountain.

"Revnik!"

Rozhdestvenskiy turned around, calling to his aide.

"Yes, Comrade Colonel?"

"Revnik. You will finish your duties here as quickly as possible, then take one hundred men to the access corridor leading to the particle beam installations atop the mountain. I estimate that the force will split into two groups — of necessity if nothing else. Your force will anticipate this, lie in wait and when a portion of the invasion group makes their way to the particle beam weapons, you will counter them, destroy them. I will personally command the motorcycle detachment and the assault vans, to cut them off at the cryogenics laboratory. They cannot be more than five minutes ahead of us and I can take my force by the most direct route. Do not hesitate to call up reinforcements should they be required. I want all but the American doctor and Major Tiemerovna dead. If there is any way, these two individuals should you encounter them are to be brought to me."

Revnik saluted. "Yes, Comrade Major."

"Yes," Rozhdestvenskiy nodded.

He began to walk toward the third garage, the doorway nearly moved aside now, reaching it, picking his way over the rubble beside the door, over the remains of bodies blown to bits and pieces.

But his car was perfect. He stared at it a moment.

He had had the country scoured for one that was both intact and had all of the equipment he needed. The Pontiac Firebird Trans-Am black, the interior black as well. Rather than the standard engine, the 308 cubic inch V-8 had the high output option, giving it 190 horsepower. Five speed transmission. He had found the best mechanic in the Womb and had the engine modified for even greater speed. Because of that, fuel economy was nil, but the Firebird would hit 150 miles per hour and stay there if it had to. There were two sets of keys for it, one locked in the wall safe in his office. The other in his hand now as he approached it. The suspension had been built up. The car was not armored, but the original equipment glass had been replaced by bullet resistant glass, dark tinted, nearly matching the black body of the car.

He opened the door, climbing into the cockpit, strapping himself in with the lap and shoulder restraint. He placed the key in the ignition, working the combination lock so he could start the machine. He turned the key—the engine roared to life ahead of him, around him. A case rested on the seat next to him—he opened it. Inside was the Uzi submachinegun, with it in neat compartments cut into the styrofoam were four thirty-two round magazines.

He depressed the top round in each of the magazines, getting the feel for the spring pressure.

It seemed adequate. He flicked on the radio hitting the PA switch. "This is Rozhdestvenskiy. I wish the twelve members of the motorcycle force to ride before me in a wedge, two man center, fifty yards ahead. I wish the four assault vans to follow behind me—two abreast. We shall follow the most direct route to the cryogenics laboratory. In the event that we should encounter the doctor or Major Tiemerovna, they are to be taken alive if at all possible so that I may deal with them personally. Rourke doubtlessly is riding my motorcycle—he has a passion for these machines. If my motorcycle must be destroyed in order to apprehend or kill him, it is of no concern. I shall advise you of my orders via the public address system. Move out in sixty seconds—from now."

He set down the microphone, closing the driver's side door, locking it, revving the huge V-8, the stick in neutral.

One by one, twelve of his Elite KGB Force mounted their

pecially selected, specially tuned Honda Gold Wings. In he rearview mirror, he could see the vans filling with their personnel, the roof panels opening, the RPK light machine-guns being elevated into position.

The bikes were starting.

He stomped the heavy duty clutch and slipped into first gear, deactivating the parking brake, feeding gasoline to the machine.

He glanced to his watch.

Forty-five seconds. All his men were mounted. "We shall take the left outside the garage and then the first right into the main traffic corridor. Maintain constant speed of fifty miles per hour until further notice." The sweep second hand of the Gold Rolex President reached the twelve.

"Move out!"

The bikes, two by two left the garage, the rumble of the machines almost deafening, the sound of his own mighty engine almost lost. He made the left, the wedge of one dozen KGB bikers ahead of him forming, his speedometer needle to fifty, staying there.

He always considered himself to have a flair for the dramatic, noting it as the four assault vans turned out of the garage and closed behind him into the formation. He reached across to the glove compartment and took from it a cassette tape, punching it into the deck, flipping the switch for the PA interlock so the tape would play out through the PA system yet he could cut it off when he spoke to issue commands.

The song the tape began to play was the Soviet national anthem.

Chapter Forty-eight

They had finished mining the last of the electric gol
carts. According to the information Natalia's uncle ha
provided, they were at the terminus of the underground an
aboveground passageways. They had encountered resist
ance along the way but had been able to shoot their wa
past.

Nine of Reed's men survived along with Reed. Ten of Vla
dov's men.

Rourke, Natalia beside him, stood overlooking Natali
and Vladov's handiwork with the last of the golf carts.

Reed spoke. "If this is the terminus between the cryogen
ics lab and the particle beam installation, then this is wher
we part company, Rourke. We're runnin' out of time. Al
this creep Rozhdestvenskiy has to do is get lucky and inter
cept us in one of the passageways with a vastly superio
force and we're goners. I'm taking my men up top to knoc
out the particle beam weapons."

"My assigned task, I believe," Vladov said, "is the de
struction of the cryogenics laboratory."

"If either group is successful," Natalia began, "The KGI
master plan will be severely damaged."

"If both groups are successful, we'll knock 'em out of th
box," Rourke nodded. "All right, we split up. Natalia and
are heading for the cryogenics lab—if somehow I can ge
some of those cryogenic chambers and enough of the se
rum, well—maybe there's a chance for my family to surviv
this. I'll give you the location of the Retreat, Reed—yo
can—"

"I'm never getting out of here alive. I walked in her

knowing that. I think Captain Vladov feels the same way. The more of these KGB assholes we kill, well, the bigger the smile on my face when the bullet finds me."

"My sentiments as well, Colonel," Vladov smiled.

"You can't say that," Rourke told Reed. "You might make it out—"

"I'd head back for Texas if I did. KGB units and Army units under their control should be pounding hell out of our boys right now."

"And I," Vladov smiled. "Someone must stay behind to destroy all that is in here, so that if some of mankind does survive, no one will be able to use this place and the material here to establish himself as a dictator. No, once the primary mission is finished, we shall continue to sabotage all that can be destroyed here in the Womb."

Rourke extended his hand to Reed. "I won't lie and say I've enjoyed knowing you, but I respect you. Good luck, and God bless you, too." Reed took his hand, nodding, saying nothing.

Vladov extended his hand to Reed. "Colonel, I think at least we are fully allies."

Reed's eyes flickered, and then he released Rourke's hand and took Vladov's. "Captain, my sincerest respect to you, to Lieutenant Daszrozinski, your men. Godspeed, Captain."

"And to you, Colonel." Vladov took a step back and saluted. Reed hesitated, then drew himself up and returned the salute, holding it for a long moment, then dropping it, Vladov turning away and walking back toward the pickup truck.

Reed looked at them, at Rourke and Natalia beside him. Reed said, "I never figured either of you. Figured Rourke was crazy for not jumpin' your bones, Major—no offense. I would have. So I guess that's a compliment. And you, Rourke—so fuckin' independent, always so damned right, so damned perfect. I guess about the best compliment I can

153

give—and I mean it—you're a good American and we could've used more like you."

Natalia took two hesitant steps forward, leaned up and kissed Reed on the cheek. Reed looked at her and smiled. "Major, if you don't mind a dying man getting his last request?"

She didn't answer him. Reed put his hands on her upper arms and drew her toward him, then kissed her full on the lips. Rourke watched as she kissed him back. "I was right all along," Reed smiled, letting go of her. "Rourke—he was crazy all this time, lady," and Colonel Reed turned away and started to walk—quickly, erect—toward the knot of his men ten yards away. He never looked back.

Chapter Forty-nine

Chambers ducked his head down, the lip of the trench blowing away, dirt and rocks showering him. He clenched his M-16 in his fists, ducking back under the sheltered portion of the redoubt, "Halversen," he shouted, calling to the radio man at the far end of the bunker. "Halversen!"

"Mr. President, nothing yet. I've tried every frequency that the KGB hasn't jammed. If the Texans are coming, sir—well, they aren't receiving us at all and I'm not picking up any of their talk."

Chambers turned away, rasping, "Keep trying, Halversen."

Footsteps along the trench, Chambers looking up, a young man in Air Force fatigues running in. "Where the hell's the president?"

"Who wants him, Sergeant?"

"My lieutenant told me to run over here. The last of the surface to air missiles was fired." There was the sound of an explosion from outside, then more gunfire. "They send any more of them damn MiG airplanes against our position, we're goners."

"They send too many more against this whole Army, we're goners."

"Where the hell's the president—supposed to tell him personally."

"Be back in a minute," Chambers said, glancing toward Halversen, but the radio man's head was leaned toward his machine.

"Probably off stickin' his head in some goddamned hole figurin' he's gonna get shot."

"Or maybe he dressed up like a woman and tried to escape through the lines, like Santa Anna did after he lost to Houston at the Battle of San Jacinto."

The Air Force sergeant laughed. "Naw, everything I hear, well—Chambers—he's a good old boy, even for a scientist, or a president. But I gotta find him though. Lieutenant wants to know what to do."

"You found him, son, I'm the president."

"You—why—" and the young Air Force sergeant—he looked barely older than nineteen—but promotion had come fast during the weeks since the Night of The War—snapped to attention. "I'm sorry, sir—I—"

"You tell your lieutenant that when the SAMs are gone to get every man in his battery to pick up an assault rifle off one of the men who's already dead. When the Russian planes come, have him have all of you fire in volleys toward the weapons pods underneath the wings. If the weapons are armed and you get a lucky hit, you might activate a detonator and blow up the damned plane. Move out, Sergeant."

"Yes, sir," and the man started to go, then turned back. "I'm sorry for what I said, Mr. President, about the damn hole and all—"

"It was a goddamned hole—and no offense taken—good luck, Sergeant," and as the sergeant started out of the bunker, Chambers found his cigarettes and his matches, lighting up. He read the warning on the side of the package and laughed out loud.

Chapter Fifty

There were a large number of "lake-worthy" craft still about, Maus had known that from his work in the Resistance and, as he stood up to survey his armada as it moved shoreward, what he saw only confirmed it. He had never stopped to count the number of craft. Marty had counted them but never told him the number.

He waved his right hand high, across the distance separating the small cabin cruiser in which he rode from the motorized sailboat in which Stanonik stood. Behind them, around them, there were more than a hundred craft—from large sailing boats to motorized launches, men and women of the Resistance, civilians who had helped but never before fought, the few survivors of Ft. Sheridan and Great Lakes.

As the ranking surviving military man, command had fallen to him. He watched as Marty—his Python in his right fist—waved back.

For the several hundred men and women, there were fewer than one hundred M-16s, some of these not originally military assault rifles at all but after-market altered from the commercial civilian model, these by the wide range of gun tinkerers Maus had collected around him into the Resistance after the Night of The War. For the most part, pistols, the dreaded "handgun" that so many had fought to eradicate from the American scene and which since the Night of The War had helped to hold the Russians back however slightly. That Americans could be armed—unlike the citizens of many nations of the world—had proven an ultimate blessing in combating the Soviet invaders. Some shotguns, some .22 rifles.

Not a machinegun among them. Not a LAWS rocket. Not even a subgun. These that they had over the course of their battles stolen from the Soviets who had stolen them from U.S. military armories, had been sent with the bulk of the Resistance toward Texas to help combat the fight against the Soviet forces massing against U.S. II. Maus and the other Resistance leaders had known that reaching Texas in time was impossible, but necessary. If sufficient forces started climbing up the backs of the Russians, they would have to divert troops from their main objective, buying time for U.S. II, however little.

The lake shore lay ahead.

Already, Soviet patrol boats were steaming toward them.

Maus raised the loud-hailer to his lips. "This is Maus. All right, they're coming to meet us. Most of us won't get through—but we knew that. Those of us that make it to shore—well, they know where we're headed. Forget about Soviet headquarters. We attack the prisoner compounds at Soldier's Field and nearby. Free as many Americans as we can. And kill as many of the Soviet troops as we have to. Good luck."

And under his breath, as he set down the loud hailer, he whispered a prayer.

In less than a minute, as he judged it, the Soviet forces would open fire.

Chapter Fifty-one

They moved on foot, running, the corridor as wide as a four lane highway, overlit by long fluorescent tubes, the corridor itself more like a seemingly endless tunnel, leading slightly upward, Reed and his men holding their rifles at high port, hugging both sides of the corridor wall, Reed leading one element, Sergeant Dressler the second element.

There were numerous side passages, but Reed wanted to keep going up, toward the particle beam weapons at the top of the mountain. Paralleling the corridor on each side was a walkway perhaps five feet higher than the main corridor surface, the walkway itself little more than six feet wide, a metal railing at the lip.

The tunnel-like corridor curved, not only upward but in a gradual spiral as best Reed could tell — it was taking him to the right place.

The absence of resistance of any kind bothered him, but also reassured him.

The KGB had second-guessed the reason for penetrating the Womb. It meant they were concentrating their efforts on the particle beam facilities and the cryogenic laboratory. It at least meant, Reed thought, that he would have a chance of nearing his goal. And once he was near to it, then he could get to it.

The men who would guard the cryogenic laboratory — if they knew the extent of the plans for the Womb — would be desperate men, fighting for their continued existence. But the men who guarded the particle beam facility were only guarding a massive weapon.

Desperation would be on Reed's side.

To a man, his soldiers were resigned to death and committed to victory. With men like these he could cut through any resistance, he told himself. If one man only could reach the facility there could be a way of turning such massive power against itself.

He thought of Rourke and laughed. Rourke who always planned ahead. Rourke had never said, "If you don't knock out the particle beam weapons I'll never get any of the cryogenic chambers or any of the serum out of here. They'll blow my aircraft out of the sky."

Rourke had never said that, but to Reed it was implicit in his understanding of the situation. That at least some of Rourke's people survive. If somehow some of the Russians survived in the Womb, or even survived vicariously through five centuries of breeding underground in the Womb, someone would need to be alive to warn the returning Eden Project, to tell the story of what happened.

To give the story of the valiant dead on both sides. That thought surprised him—to consider a Russian valiant. But Ravitski had been brave, had died. Vladov, Daszrozinski and the others would die.

It was only fitting that someone survive to remember them.

Reed walked on, the corridor taking a sharp bend, upward and angling left. They were nearing their goal—and nearing death.

Reed slipped his hand under his fatigue blouse. There was a ziploc plastic bag there, folded inside it an American flag. He had a planned use for it.

Chapter Fifty-two

Rourke slowed the fire engine red Kawasaki Ninja, making a wide circle as he stopped, swinging the M-16 forward on its sling, keeping the Ninja's engine running under him.

Natalia, at the wheel of the Ford pickup, slowed, stopped. Vladov, riding beside her, jumped out, shouting something to Daszrozinski in the truck bed, Daszrozinski and the nine other men of the SF unit and Major Gorki and Sergeant Druszik of GRU evacuating the truck bed as well.

Rourke stared down the corridor. It was as wide as a four lane highway, a walkway on each side just about the width of a car, a railing running the length of the corridor. Overhead, banks of fluorescent tubes glowed brightly, giving an almost green tinge to everything the light touched.

"There it is," Rourke almost whispered, squinting against the light and gesturing along the length of the corridor. The corridor ended some two hundred yards ahead, and beyond it would be the cryogenics lab.

"They are waiting for us," Vladov observed.

"Yeah, I figured that, too," Rourke nodded. He took the .45 from his belt, snapped back the slide and let it run forward. He upped the safety and stuffed the pistol back in his belt. The grip safety had never been pinned or otherwise deactivated—if the thumb safety should wipe off, the gun was still at least marginally safe to carry that way.

"There is no way to go around them," Natalia called, climbed down from the cab of the pickup. "At least if we want to reach the lab."

"They'll let us get close enough, then open up, most likely."

"Doctor," Vladov began. "I view our mission — meaning by that the mission of myself and my men — I view it that we have the primary goal of getting yourself and Major Tiemerovna inside the cryogenics laboratory, to destroy the supplies of the cryogenic serum and perhaps to steal some for use at your Retreat, along with the appropriate cryogenics chambers and monitoring equipment. That being the case, we shall go ahead, forming a corridor for yourself and the major through which you can penetrate the laboratory. After that, I'm afraid the rest shall be left in the capable hands of yourself and the major. We shall be otherwise engaged."

"Let's get this straight for once and for all. I want to save my family, but my primary mission is to prevent Rozhdestvenskiy's people from sleeping through the holocaust and awakening to destroy the Eden Project — when and if it returns."

"And if it doesn't, Doctor, you should consider that. If we succeed in destroying the utility of the Womb, but do not succeed in saving your family, then it will all have been meaningless if the Eden Project should fail to return. I know little about space travel, aside from the exploits of our Soviet cosmonauts, aside from the few American films I have seen when for a time I served as military attache to our embassy in Japan. But I understand that quite a few things could go wrong. A malfunction in the onboard electrical systems could cause the cryogenic chambers inside the shuttles to cease to function. The occupants would die. A meteor shower could attack the ships and destroy them. If the mathematical calculations were incorrect, rather than an elliptical orbit taking them to the edge of the solar system and back again, they might instead drift out of the solar system and voyage endlessly. When they awaken, they would be doomed to wander forever, if they chose to return to their sleep, or they would die in a matter of hours when shipboard oxygen was depleted. In other words, the sur-

162

vival of your family, though I have never met them, is vital. Without their survival, if we succeed, we will have achieved nothing. There will be no human race. All mankind would be lost."

"Some people may survive, living underground, if they're smart enough and technologically set —"

"Another maybe. Whereas, the mountain Retreat General Varakov has spoken of should be impervious, the electrical supply you yourself saying should likely be infinite. There is an Americanism, I believe — the best wager —"

"Best bet," Rourke corrected automatically.

"Very well, your family is the best bet for the survival of the human race. That is the priority which my general has given me, and which I shall obey. Perhaps, if you do survive, and in the era five centuries from now you should help to rebuild cities and towns," and Vladov smiled, almost sheepishly, "I would find it amusing. In the Soviet Army, my particular unit has earned the name Drahka — it simply means in English —"

"Fight," Rourke interrupted.

"Yes. It sums up our lives, our destinies, our spirit, our honor, that we never give up. Perhaps — well — a street, or a village square where children play — it might somehow be something we would somehow know."

Rourke swallowed hard, then nodded.

"After all, a Russian name, a Russian word in an American town — it might be very amusing."

"I shouldn't think it would be amusing — but it would be fitting," Rourke nodded.

"Comrade Doctor, I understand Daszrozinski has called you this once and you did not find it an offense. For in truth we are the best comrades, all of us in this fight."

"Comrade Captain, Zehlahyou Udahchee," Rourke murmured.

"Comrade Doctor, good luck," Vladov echoed. He extended his right hand — Rourke took it. Vladov stepped back. He turned to Natalia. He called his men to attention, the GRU major and sergeant snapping to as well. He raised his hand in salute to her, "Comrade Major. Your uncle was and always shall be our nation's finest officer. On behalf of your uncle and yourself, please accept our salute." He called to the other Russians, "Present arms!"

Natalia stood for a moment—Rourke thought she was about to weep. But she raised her right hand—it was the last salute she would ever give, he knew, however it worked out. She held it. Finally, Vladov commanded, "Order arms," and the rifle salutes went down. Vladov nodded to her, "Comrade Major," and lowered his salute. She lowered hers.

And as Rourke watched her, now she did weep.

Chapter Fifty-three

Of the armada, only some two dozen of the ships remained, Maus hauling himself up from the waves, his left arm bloody and useless to him, a .45 in his right fist as he ordered his legs to move him forward. KBG troops, ahead of him, to his right, less than a half dozen of the Resistance coming out of the water with him. He fired the .45, taking down one of the KGB men. For a moment he thought of his wife. He swallowed hard, firing again, slugs tearing into the rocks near him, one of the Resistance fighters going down, screaming.

Maus stood his ground, stabbing the .45 ahead of him, firing.

A searing pain in his left leg and he stumbled forward, falling hard against the rocks, firing the pistol as soon as he raised it, another of the KGB men going down.

"Hang on, Tommy!"

The voice almost made him laugh. The boom of a .357 Magnum, again and again and again, the thunder of a shotgun, then again.

He looked to his left.

It was Marty, the Python in his fist, another man beside him holding a riot shotgun.

Marty dropped to his knees beside him. "You okay, Tommy?"

"Am I okay? You crazy. My left arm's almost shot off and somebody shot my left leg out from under me, but I'll make it. Get me up. We're headin' for Soldiers Field. How many of us left?"

"Maybe fifty, scattered all over the shoreline for

about a city block. Seven of the Russian patrol boats are left."

"The hell with 'em—let's move—get me up," and Marty hauled Maus's right arm across his shoulders, Maus getting to his feet, wincing from the pain in his left leg. But he could hobble.

"All those times I told ya, without me you'd be flat on your face—took this to make you see it seriously," Marty laughed.

"All right. So walk already. In my next life I'll treat you better." Moving made him scream inside himself, but he forced the pain from his mind as much as he could. There were Americans who needed to be freed before they died.

They reached the height of the spit of land near the airfield, Marty discharging the Python twice more, downing one of the KGB men.

The man with the shotgun on Maus's left picked up the AKM and handed Maus the shotgun. "Can you hold it with your left hand enough to use it like a cane—it's outa ammo anyway." Maus took it, his left arm barely able to move, but he closed the fingers of his left fist around it, supporting his left leg now rather than just dragging it.

"I can walk," Maus snarled, Marty letting free of his right arm, reloading the Python.

"So you can walk—how about shoot?"

"Put a fresh magazine in for me and we'll see, huh?"

Marty took the Colt from Maus's right hand, dumped the spent magazine—the slide locked open already—and took the magazine from the single carrier on Maus's belt. He rammed it home, letting the slide run forward, upping the safety, handing the Colt back to Maus.

"So let's kill some KGB guys and free those Americans and if there's time before the sky catches on fire I'll let you buy me a beer," Marty laughed.

"Sounds okay to me—but you can buy—I bought the last time."

Together they walked ahead. And somehow, the fighting around them sporadic, more of the Resistance forming around them, he felt they'd make it.

Chapter Fifty-four

Lieutenant Feltcher peered through the binoculars. Below him the Western Soviet Army, far in the distance the Eastern Army. No one bothered with his aircraft and he ordered the pilot to veer off, replacing the binoculars in their case and picking up the microphone. It was all in a nonsense code he had worked out, something the KGB would not decipher quickly. "This is organ grinder, calling taffy pull, over."

The voice came back immediately. "Taffy pull to organ grinder—reading you. Go ahead. Over."

"Affirm right testicle and left—your nearest moving. Farthest coming up with a birthday party—getting my drift? Over."

"Affirmative, organ grinder—come home for a snack. Taffy pull out."

"Organ grinder out."

Taffy pull was the TVM—Texas Volunteer Militia. Surprise Party meant unexpected forces behind the Eastern Soviet Army—Resistance as best Feltcher could make out, perhaps from states all over the southeast and middle west. He had no way to tell. But there were at least a thousand vehicles coming up behind the Eastern Soviet Army.

The reference to testicles had meant the Armies themselves—the right one the Army of the West, the left the Army of the East. U.S. II forces were in the distance as he stared back across the terrain. A certain sadness overwhelmed him. The Resistance Army about to assault the rear of the Soviet Army of the East had crossed through the no-man's land of the Mississippi, intentionally exposing themselves to radiation, sealing their death.

But they came anyway. Soon, the Soviet Armies wouldn't know what hit them.

"Make this thing fly faster, huh. I don't wanna miss Armageddon by five minutes."

The snack — it meant the attack was about to begin.

Chapter Fifty-five

Vladov and his men had moved ahead, to confront the enemy at the end of the corridor which led to the cryogenics lab, Natalia standing beside Rourke, watching with him as Vladov moved on. Behind them, at the far end of the corridor, Rourke knew there would be a cordon of KGB Elite Corps — to block any possible retreat.

But it was quiet for a moment, Natalia saying, "Have I brought all of this upon you, John?"

Rourke folded her into his arms, drawing her head to his chest. "No, no more than I brought it on you. If you'd never met me, Karamatsov would probably still be alive and he'd be running the show here and you'd have a place in the Womb."

"I wouldn't have wanted that," she interrupted, her voice low, muffled sounding against him.

"I know that — neither would I."

"If — if Captain Vladov — what if —"

"If the Eden Project never returns and we survive somehow?"

"Yes," she answered softly.

"You'll never want," Rourke told her.

She looked up at him, Rourke touching the tips of his fingers to her chin, looking into her eyes, their incredible blueness. When Vladov and his men had first moved out, she had changed into her own clothes — her battle gear, a black jumpsuit. Rourke too had changed out of the borrowed Soviet uniform, to his faded Levis, his combat boots, a light blue chambray shirt, his battered brown leather bomber jacket covering the twin Detonics stainless pistols.

"I'll always love you," he told her, pulling her closer against him, kissing her, his mouth crushing against hers.

"We might be better off—all of us—if I died here," she said.

Rourke pushed her away, his fingers clamped tight to her upper arms. "Don't you say that, don't ever say that. Life isn't something you can throw away—not a life like yours. Don't ever think that. Because if you die here, I'd fight here until the last one of them was dead or I was dead. And then all of this would be for nothing."

There were tears in her eyes. "But you already have a wife, and you are not the kind of man to—"

"No—I'm not," Rourke told her. "You've trusted me. And I've trusted you. You have to trust me in this," Rourke almost whispered.

"I read the fairy tale about sleeping beauty when I was a girl—my uncle would bring things to me from all over the world. It was a beautiful book—I think it was printed in America. He taught me English because he said I must know the way my potential enemy would think and could not unless I understood his language. But—with the cryogenic sleep—will you," and she smiled, turning her face away, her lips touching at his right hand.

Rourke drew her to him. "Awaken you with a kiss?" And he held her very close, his lips touching her hair.

He knew what he would do. Because if the Eden Project did not return, and he eradicated the Womb, six people would remain alive on earth. Perhaps others would survive through the generations. But what five centuries of incalculable hardship would have wrought was something incomprehensible to him. There would only, perhaps, be six. Michael, Annie, Paul, Sarah, Natalia and himself.

He very much wanted to awaken her with a kiss, but wanting something didn't always make it so. But he kissed her now, harder than he had ever kissed her.

171

Chapter Fifty-six

Rourke sat astride the Ninja, the gas tank nearly full, the motor throbbing beneath him, the bike almost as if it possessed a will of its own and wanted to move ahead and be done with the waiting.

He looked at Natalia in the cab of the olive drab Ford pickup truck.

She nodded.

Rourke had taken a second M-16, one suspended now from each side of his body. All of his guns were checked, speedloaders loaded, magazines full, knives in position on his body and sharp.

"Ready," he called to Natalia. Vladov's men were in position. The shooting would start in an instant and he had no intention of letting them give their lives just to get him and Natalia past. He would kill as many of the KGB Elite Corps as he could along the way.

"I love you, John Thomas Rourke."

"I love you. Let's go," and Rourke saw her blue eyes one more time, then gunned the fire engine red Kawasaki Ninja ahead, the pickup moving to his left, the tunnel-like corridor walls speeding past him, the lights overhead a blur of green light.

Both of the M-16s were charged, the safeties set, and Rourke, as the Ninja sped under him, shifted one of them slightly forward, the butt hitting against the seat. He moved the selector to auto—ready. His pack was in the truck cab beside Natalia. So was the CAR-15.

He wore his sunglasses—they cut the glare of the overhead lighting and protected his eyes from the slipstream over the low faring.

Under his breath, he gave a near silent challenge. "You try, Rozhdestvenskiy, you try real hard to stop me, asshole."

The shooting had begun near the end of the corridor.

John Rourke rode the machine straight toward it.

Chapter Fifty-seven

Vladov's men were pinned at the corridor and, brilliantly bright light beyond and the KGB Elite Corps there. Rourke knew Rozhdestvenskiy would be there, too.

He gunned the Ninja, shifting the M-16 forward, clutching it at the pistol grip, his right index finger along the side of the guard, ready to move against the trigger. Natalia was perhaps twenty yards behind him, Rourke holding the Ninja back, Natalia giving the truck all the gas she could, he knew.

He moved his right index finger into the trigger guard, barely touching at the Colt assault rifle's trigger.

Natalia had said that aboard the bike he would be like horsemounted cavalry—hit hard and run through, he thought.

The enemy was ahead. Vladov's men cheered as he passed, leaving their positions, running, their AKS-74 assault rifles blazing, their full dress uniforms resplendent with their medals, pride etched across their faces as they ran to the attack.

Rourke opened fire, the corridor gone now, a wide, high, long and vaulted chamber surrounding him, KGB Elite Corps forces behind packing crates, overturned golf carts, atop metal ribbed construction towers to each die. Rourke worked the M-16's trigger in even three round bursts, aiming the Ninja toward the greatest concentration of the KGB, and the cryogenics laboratory beyond.

The M-16 was empty, bodies falling to it as he let it fall to his right side, his right hand snatching the Python from the leather at his hip, the big Colt thrusting forward, his right index finger double actioning it—the face of one of the KGB men to his right exploded. Rourke fired again—one of the KGB Elite Corps guards in one of the metal ribbed construction towers, his body tumbling downward, the M-16 in his hands spraying death into his own comrades. Rourke fired again, an Elite Corpsman hurtling his body at the bike—the man's neck seemed to dissolve into red at the adam's apple.

Rourke fired again, among them now, gutshooting one of them. He fired again, an Elite Corpsman lunging toward him with a bayonet—the man's face exploded under the impact. He fired again—an Elite Corpsman spraying an M-16 toward him—the body sprawled back against a half dozen of his comrades.

The Python was empty. Rourke shoved it into the leather, snatching the Colt Government Model from his waistband, his right thumb wiping down the safety, his right index finger already inside the trigger guard—he fired, a 185-grain Jacketed Hollow Point impacting the forehead of one of the Elite Corpsmen—an officer—aiming a pistol toward Rourke's face.

Rourke swerved the Ninja, plowing toward the main KGB position again, heading straight for the center of them, emptying the .45 ahead of him into targets of opportunity, ramming the pistol—the action still open, into his waistband.

His right hand found the little Detonics under his right armpit, jerking it free awkwardly, his right thumb jacking back the hammer, his index finger working the trigger, another Elite Corpsman down.

Vladov's men were closing on the position, shouts coming from them, Natalia ramming the nose of the pickup truck into a knot of the Elite Corpsmen—screams of the dying drowning the rattle of gunfire.

Rourke fired out the little Detonics .45, the lives he claimed lost to him. He stuffed the pistol into his right hip pocket, drawing the identical gun from the holster under his left armpit, cocking the hammer, firing, killing, firing, killing, firing, killing. He swerved the bike—almost losing it from under him—and aimed the bike toward them again. Natalia's truck was reversing at high speed, men running from it.

Beside him nearly, one of Vladov's men rammed a bayonet into the throat of one of the Elite Corpsmen.

Rourke fired out the little Detonics, killing more of them.

He stuffed the pistol into his belt, reaching behind him— the Metalifed two-inch Colt Lawman. He doubled actioned the .357, the flash brilliant, the target a face inches from him, his wrist feeling the recoil hard, the skin of the face catching fire for an instant as the Elite Corpsman fell back dead.

More of the Elite Corps coming from the corridor.

Vladov shouted, "Get out of here, Doctor. You and the major must be about your business."

Rourke slowed the bike, making an arc with it, thrusting the little Lawman ahead of him, emptying the cylinder into the bodies of KGB Elite Corpsmen around him.

Natalia had the truck moving forward again, KGB clinging to it.

Rourke stuffed the little Lawman into its holster at the small of his back, dumping the spent magazine in the M-16 at his right side, replacing it, swinging both Colt assault rifles forward, firing them simultaneously, cutting the KGB bodies from the sides of her vehicle, cutting them away, excising them like he would cut away a tumor with a scalpel. He let both rifles fall to his sides, both magazines half spent, the safeties on.

"Vladov, God bless you!"

"And you!" Rourke gunned the Ninja, making a wide arc with it, Natalia already driving the pickup past the KGB position, toward the far end of the chamber. The cryogenics lab was there, Rourke knew.

176

A KGB Elite Corpsman jumped for the bike—Rourke drew the big Gerber from its sheath and hacked him down, riding on.

Chapter Fifty-eight

The fighting for the moment was all behind them. At the far end of the vaulted room was another corridor, short by comparison to the ones through which they had passed.

Rourke shouted to Natalia, "Stop for a minute."

The truck began to slow, Rourke arcing the bike under him, bringing it to a halt, balancing it under him as quickly, he began reloading his weapons, introducing fresh fully loaded magazines to the assault rifles as well.

"Vladov's men are the best in the Soviet Union," Natalia called. "But he will be outnumbered at least ten to one in a few moments. He cannot hold too long against such odds."

Rourke nodded agreement. "I know, I don't think we'll encounter that much resistance at the lab itself—they wouldn't want to risk a shootout that would destroy their equipment. If we get inside, we should be able to get loaded and get out again before we bump into more trouble." He loaded the last of the two revolvers—the Python—and holstered it.

"Let's go," and Rourke gunned the Ninja. He looked back once.

Vladov and his men were holding the chamber. The sound of gunfire was loud. Soon it would reach a peak, then stop—and Vladov and his men—they would be dead. Capture for them was something Rourke didn't even consider.

"Let's get out of here," and Rourke started into the corridor.

Chapter Fifty-nine

Five of his men lived, Daszrozinski though wounded, among them. Both of the GRU men had perished in the fighting.

"I have not seen, Comrade Captain—I have not seen Colonel Rozhdestvenskiy."

"He is here somewhere. Perhaps ahead, waiting for Doctor Rourke and Comrade Major Tiemerovna near the laboratory. But he is here."

The fighting had slowed for a moment, the Elite Corps personnel massing by the long corridor through which Vladov and his men had come, Elite Corps bodies littering the floor, dangling dead or dying from the construction towers.

"I believe that we should counterattack, my friend," Vladov smiled. His own wounded side hurt him badly and he had lost considerable blood and his head ached from it.

"Yes, Comrade Captain, I believe this, too, when they come for us, we can go to them. We can show them what it really means to be Russian."

"Order the men to check their weapons and fix bayonets."

Vladov blotted out Daszrozinski's response, staring across the overturned golf cart toward the KGB Elite Corps position by the end of the corridor. He checked his Smith & Wesson automatics—all three of them, one at a time.

He checked his rifle. He affixed the inverted Bowie bladed bayonet to it.

"Comrade Captain, we are ready," Daszrozinski said, interrupting Vladov's thoughts—of death and what, if anything, lay beyond it. It was easier to die, he considered, as someone other than a Russian. One might be allowed to grow up with a faith in some afterlife. But nothing about being Russian was easy or ever had been. And he was proud somehow of that.

He looked at his men.

"When they come for us, we shall cheat them, we shall counterattack. I estimate there are one hundred of them massing there by the end of the corridor. There are six of us. We should easily be able to kill one quarter of their number, perhaps greater than that. For we are whom we are, we are the best our nation has to offer. We are the finest soldiers who have ever lived. We have trained, we have fought, some of us have already died. And the rest shall join our comrades soon. If any of you hold a religious belief, now is the time to make your peace with your God. This will be the last battle for us all. I have never known finer comrades—there could be no finer comrades for any officer, for any man."

Vladov extended his right hand to each of his men in turn, all of them huddled there behind the overturned golf carts. At last he came to Daszrozinski. "My finest friend," he told the younger officer. The two men embraced.

Vladov had cried once before in his adult life, when the woman he had been about to marry had died in an agricultural accident.

He cried now as he raised his right hand to salute his men. Each returned the salute.

From the end of the corridor across the space of the vaulted hall from them there was a shout. Then the sound of an automatic weapon.

He lowered the salute as did his men.

He looked across the golf carts—the KGB Elite Corps

was walking forward, their weapons firing sporadically.

"See to your uniforms," Vladov ordered, the men straightening their tunics. "Gloves." Each man in turn took his parade dress white gloves from inside his uniform, pulling them on. Vladov straightened his beret.

"A wedge formation—we run to them—we kill them. My comrades."

Vladov raised himself up—his side hurt him terribly, but he kept his head up.

"Attack—fight!" He started to run forward, Daszrozinski beside him, his men around him. He fired out the AKS-74, seeing it all as if in slow motion when the Elite Corps bodies fell to his fire. He let the assault rifle fall to his side. His 659 pistols—both 9mms in his hands, he ran ahead, emptying the double column magazines at his enemies. Daszrozinski fell beside him and did not move, dead.

He kept going, both pistols emptied—he let them fall from his hands—he would not need them in an anonymous mass grave with his comrades. He drew the Smith Mini Gun in the shoulder holster under his tunic, firing, killing, another of his men down, a scream issuing from his throat, "Long live the—" But he died before the word came out.

Vladov moved ahead, walking now, his pistol empty—he let it fall. He raised his empty rifle—no time to load it, closing with the KGB, his bayonet doing its mighty work, hacking, slashing, killing. The rifle fell from his right hand as the fingers there were severed.

His men were dead.

He grabbed his knife with his left hand, unsheathing it, burying it in the chest of an Elite Corps Major—killing him.

He felt the coldness suddenly, not knowing for an instant if it were the blood loss, the shock, or the moment before death.

It was the moment before death he realized then, a bayonet being ripped from his already wounded side as he fell.

But in Vladov's left hand was the knife. The bayonet stabbed at him again, missing him, Vladov thrusting the knife upward, into the abdomen of his attacker. There was a scream.

The blades of perhaps a dozen bayonets hacked toward him and Vladov shouted the name given his men and himself. "Fight!" One of the blades was coming at his throat and he didn't turn his face away from it and . . .

Chapter Sixty

Reed fired the last round from his .45 into the face of the KGB Elite Corpsman, shoving the body aside, pushing against the doorway — it didn't give. But Dressler was beside him, rasping, "Stay back, sir," and Dressler's M-16 emptied into the locking mechanism.

Reed threw his body against the doors, his left shoulder aching him badly, his left arm already drenched with his blood.

The doors gave and Reed half fell through, Dressler beside him. They threw their bodies against the doors, closing them, the fighting still going on in the corridor outside, less than a half dozen of Reed's men surviving it.

"Sir, you goin' up to the particle beam weapons?"

"I'm gonna sabotage the controls. President Chambers told me what to do if I got this far — make the power build up in the system and blow the weapons up — "

"You gonna be needin' me, Colonel. I'd sorta — well — the men outside there."

"Gimme your plastique, Sergeant Dressler."

Dressler reached under his fatigue blouse. "Here, sir — nice and warm. Malleable."

Reed nodded, noticing for the first time that in the battle to get out of the smaller access corridor, Dressler too had been wounded — his left leg was drenched with blood and there was a wound from the right side of his neck, blood clotting there.

Reed gave his hand to Dressler. "Sergeant, God bless, huh?"

"You, too, sir, if'n you're plannin' to blow this door, you'll never get out."

"And they'll never get in, Sarge," and Reed made himself laugh.

"Be seein' ya, Colonel."

"Right — for sure — be seein' ya," and Dressler ripped the door open and was gone, Reed hearing the gunfire, then throwing his body against the doors. He dropped to his knees, molding the C-4 against the door frame — he had to cause part of the wall to collapse. This would block the door. A gunshot would be the detonator. He worked quickly — his men would soon be dead and the Elite Corps would be at the door — and at his heels.

Chapter Sixty-one

He had ridden the motorcycle up the ramp onto the small loadng dock beside the cryogenics laboratory, waiting for something to happen. Nothing did. He stopped the fire engine red Ninja, dismounting then, letting down the stand.

An M-16, selector set to full auto, filled each hand.

The truck brakes—he heard them and he glanced back—Natalia had backed the pickup to the dock.

He heard the door slam and looked back again—she was out—his CAR-15 was slung across her back, an M-16 was in each hand as she turned a full three hundred sixty degrees.

"Where are they, John?"

"Inside, maybe," Rourke told her.

There had been no resistance as they had left the small corridor, no resistance as they had entered the huge concrete box which formed the chamber, the cryogenics lab. It had once been an ordinance lab, dominating the far wall.

"Perhaps they—"

"What?" Rourke asked her.

"All of their forces—perhaps they are committed there with Vladov and against Reed. Perhaps—"

"No, I don't think so." She had mounted the ramp leading from the floor level to the loading dock. She stood back to back with him now.

"What do we do?"

"We go inside—what we're expected to do, I guess."

Rourke approached the double swinging doors, padlocked from the outside. He loosed a burst from his M-16, the lock disintegrating. He took a step back, then two steps forward, a roundhouse double Tae Kwon Do kick to the center portion of the two doors, at the joint where they mated, the chain falling free, the doors swinging inward, only one swinging back. There was no gunfire, from inside, from anywhere.

"We're walking into a trap, John."

"We don't have any choice, Natalia." Rourke shoved the rifle in his right hand through the doorspace — nothing happened.

He followed the muzzle of the rifle inside. "Stay here for a second," telling Natalia.

The cryogenics laboratory's lights were lit. There was no one that he could see.

He looked up — the false ceiling was ten feet from the floor — There was no one in the vast laboratory.

"Come inside and watch the doors from here," Rourke called to Natalia.

Rourke started across the laboratory, both rifles ready in his hands.

The far wall was dominated by rows of shelves, three litre sized bottles there, the apparent color of the bottles a very pale green, like the color of Rhine wine.

"The cryogenic serum," he said under his breath. His palms sweated. He walked toward it. To his far right, as he scanned the room, were wooden packing crates, some large, the size and shape of coffins. Some smaller, like the size of a bedroom-sized color TV portable. Some of the crates were open, most were not. To his left, running as far as the extent of the laboratory, were ranks of what he judged were cryogenic chambers — translucent lids, open, some few closed, monitoring equipment rigged to them.

He started toward the cryogenic serum again.

There was a sound from above him — Rourke wheeled — the panel of ceiling overhead had slid open — the muzzles of automatic rifles pointed down at him. "Run for it, Natalia!" Rourke stabbed both M-16s upward to fire.

A voice, "Doctor Rourke, a moment, please!"

Rourke looked to his right. Near the cryogenic sleep chambers a man stood, having hidden behind them, Rourke guessed. Two dozen others stood near him, all armed. "You will die, my dear Doctor Rourke, but I first wanted to talk."

Rourke licked his lips. Natalia stood at the entrance to the laboratory, both M-16s hanging on their slings at her sides. There was something that was not right about her, but guns were pointed at her from the ceiling above and from the area near the cryogenic chambers.

More of the ceiling panels opened, men dropping down from the ceiling now, M-16s pointed toward Rourke and toward her.

"You see, Doctor, however daring your plan, it was doomed to failure," Rozhdestvenskiy smiled. "I won't degrade you both by ordering you to drop your weapons, you would not have time to use them." Natalia was walking toward him, both fists balled at her sides, the KGB Elite Corps personnel falling back from her as though somehow afraid of her.

"And you, my dear Major, what a lovely creature you have always been. And how traitorous."

"You are the traitor," Natalia barely whispered. "You, and my husband, he was like you."

"Ohh, such a way to talk, Major, about someone who is dead and can no longer champion his good name."

"His good name—his perversions, his evil, the way that he beat me—his good name indeed."

"The affairs between a husband and wife," and he smiled gesturing palms upward and shrugging. "These are not my affair, Major. But without him, there would have been no knowledge of the Eden Project, no knowledge of the cryogenic serum which allows the cryogenic sleep to save lives rather than take them—without him," and he gestured expansively around him, "none of this. He was my dear friend—though I am aware of his shortcomings. But no one is perfect. Except perhaps for you and Doctor Rourke. And you shall both soon see what perfection can profit you."

Slowly, Natalia had been moving her hands to the pistol grips of her rifles. Rourke still held both his M-16s in his fists, but a shootout would have netted nothing, he realized. He waited for Natalia—she had something, he knew that, some play ready.

Her hands were nearly to her rifles.

Rozhdestvenskiy laughed, "Major, hold your rifles if you wish, point them at me even, you will not get off a shot before you are cut down."

Natalia's hands closed on the pistol grips. "Thank you for letting me hold my rifles."

"If you draw comfort from them in these, your last moments alive, feel free, my dear. You see, we anticipated the arrival of yourself and the Doctor."

"Who?" Rourke asked suddenly.

"Ahh," Rozhdestvenskiy laughed. "Your American public television—the British television series—you have a ready wit, Doctor. But I'm afraid neither that nor anything else shall save you and the major from retribution," and he smiled ingratiatingly, obviously enjoying what he was doing.

Rourke shrugged, "All my life, you know, I've never really been able to make jokes, to make people laugh, I considered it a character flaw. But just recently, I've been doing better."

"Too bad you won't have the time to develop the talent, Doctor."

Rourke shrugged.

Natalia said nothing.

Rozhdestvenskiy continued. "We anticipated your arrival, as I indicated. The actual ceiling goes up some twenty feet. The false ceiling was installed for better temperature control. But we installed the ceiling to already existing girders which spanned the laboratory. So it was simple to position some of my men above you."

188

"Yes," Rourke nodded.

Natalia spoke. "You were very kind, Colonel, to let me hold my rifles at the pistol grips. Both rifles have their selectors set to full automatic."

"My dear, it is useless, before you raise them toward me, you'll be dead."

"But I don't have to raise them," Natalia smiled, her voice like honey. "I anticipated this would be a trap. Do you remember the C-4 explosives which we have used so efficaciously against you?"

Rozhdestvenskiy smile started to fade.

"The muzzles of both rifles are packed with one pound apiece. All I have to do is twitch my finger against either trigger and the explosions will destroy the cryogenic serum for you. It is only perhaps fifteen feet away and I doubt the glass in the bottles will withstand the shock."

"You lie — kill — "

"Try me!" She shrieked the words. No one moved.

"You would not — "

"Why not," Rourke almost whispered.

"Even if your gunfire should sever my arms from my body, the involuntary nervous responses will cause the fingers to twitch against the triggers — your serum, your life — gone."

"But — but yours, too."

"We came here for some of the cryogenic chambers and monitoring equipment, and a supply of serum for ourselves. And to destroy your serum. So you'd die when the holocaust comes. We'll settle for the first two — some of the chambers — we need six, we'll take six along with the spare parts kits, the monitoring equipment. We'll take six bottles of the serum."

"Each recipient needs only a few ccs," Rozhdestvenskiy began.

"We'll take six anyway — we'll leave the rest for you. Compromise?"

"John!"

"Leave it, Natalia. It's my plan now."

Rozhdestvenskiy licked his lips. "You'll never get out of here alive."

"You have your boys play cops and robbers with us after we load up — in fact, have them load us up — but they don't have to check the water and oil. We're just fine and the truck runs great — and I love the bike — yours?"

"Yes."

"I leave it for you. Ride around on it for the next five hundred years and have fun. I'll walk toward the doors — and grabbing me will just make Natalia blow up the serum. I'll keep an eye on the loading, make sure nobody tampers with the vehicles. And once we're loaded up, I'll aim my rifles at the serum until Natalia gets free — wouldn't want half the bottles shot up, would you? If we make a play for the rest of the serum, you've got nothing to lose by killing us. And why would we risk a gunfight after we have the serum and the chambers we need."

"Then we will meet again in five centuries, Doctor. To resume the battle, you fresh from your Retreat in the Georgia mountains if you get there and me fresh from the Womb?"

"If you get there," Rourke smiled. "And make sure your guys are real careful loading the stuff. We wouldn't want to waste any of the serum, would we?"

Natalia stood her ground.

Rourke gestured with his M-16s to the KGB men nearest the serum. "Move away, guys. The lady's gonna stand right there near the serum." As Natalia moved slowly past him, Rourke winked at her.

Chapter Sixty-two

There had been a gunbattle with the weapons crew — four men. Reed had killed them all. He leaned heavily over the controls panels now — he had been shot three times in the abdomen and was dying.

He worked the controls, knowing just enough Russian and just enough about the mechanics of a laser charged particle beam system to know which control to work, the information on the weapons system courtesy of Samuel Chambers' best scientific guesswork. Reed hoped the man had been right.

There was a loud humming noise from the vault behind him, the vault extending for perhaps a quarter mile, massive diameter tubes coiling back and forth. These were used to generate the speed for the particles which formed the beam.

He kept working the controls. There would likely be service personnel in the charging area itself — they would come to kill him. But he doubted they were armed, only one of the crewmen had been armed, and that only with a pistol.

He set the controls, using his bayonet to pry off the dials without moving the dial stems leading into the control panels. He crushed the plastic dials under the heels of his combat boots, then left the consoles, the humming a loud whine now.

He went to the entry doors, setting out more of the plastique — the last that he had — against the locking mechanism. He had destroyed the lock by hammering it out of shape with the butt of the dead Russian's American pistol. The lock would have to be shot through to enter the control room — and a shot would blow the plastique.

He returned to the control panels, picking up the 1911A1 pistol again, using the butt to hammer out the faces of gauges and digital readout panels — the numbers had been climbing steadily. The gauges were gone.

A voice from behind him — a man. A pipe wrench in both hands like a club. Reed fired into his face with the .45, killing him. Reed picked up the wrench, swinging it against the control panel, shattering the casings — the humming grew steadily louder. The fire control console — he smashed it with the wrench — there would be no way to fire and release the charged particle. Without putting a new control panel into place.

The humming, the whining was a roar now.

He wondered how long until the overloaded system would explode. Perhaps it would rip away the top of the mountain. At least it would destroy the weapons system utterly. He had read an intelligence memo about particle beam devices — similar to a neutron explosion — perhaps the life in the Womb would be destroyed as well.

He closed his eyes against the pain inside him — his abdomen, his left arm.

Reed prayed Rourke and Natalia would have the time to carry out their mission, but there was no waiting now.

No time left.

He used the wrench one more time to smash out the glass ahead of and above the control panels, the particle beam weapons stretching skyward. It was nearly dusk he realized — the last night?

Awkwardly, blood spurting between his fingers as he held in his intestines, he dragged himself across the control panels and through the opening, breaking out the rest of the glass with the slide of his .45.

The rocks below were navigable. Then perhaps a fifty yard walk to the base of the nearest gantry-like structure which housed the particle beam weapon and raised it skyward.

Before he started down from the rocks, he felt under his fatigue blouse, through the blood feeling the plastic bag which covered the flag. There would be bullet holes in it. Blood on it.

But it wouldn't be the first time. He started down the rocks and toward the gantry.

Chapter Sixty-three

The truck was loaded with six of the U.S.-made cryogenic chambers which Rourke himself had personally in-
spected as best as possible to determine their functional
capabilities. Six spare parts kits. Six monitoring equipment
kits, six spare parts kits for the monitoring equipment.

Five of the serum bottles, packed in wooden cases were
aboard the truckbed. Natalia had let one of the rifles drop
to her side and carried the sixth bottle now, Rourke standing in the doorway, both assault rifles aimed across the laboratory toward the bottles of cryogenic serum as Natalia
walked free.

Rozhdestvenskiy and a bearded man in a lab coat stood
far to one side. The KGB Elite Corps flanked her on both
sides, their rifles lowered.

Rourke spoke. "Try anything to stop Major Tiemerovna
and I empty both magazines into the serum bottles. It won't
do much good to pick it up off the floor and even if you
chemically analyze it, it'd take too long to reproduce a sufficient amount."

"They do not have the proper chemicals—my uncle told
me this. The one factory which produced the key ingredient
was destroyed during the Night of The War. The chemical
cannot be reproduced because its formula was top secret
and it is the one portion of the Eden Project plan they have
never found."

"You are so well informed, Major," Rozhdestvenskiy
shouted. "That traitorous bastard of an uncle—were there
time remaining, I would personally execute him."

She stopped walking, raising the rifle at her right side

194

slightly. "Another word about my uncle and I destroy the serum—all of it. I'm still close enough."

"Get out of here," Rozhdestvenskiy rasped.

Natalia kept walking, Rourke never moving the muzzles of the two M-16s. If he fired he would cut down Natalia as well. But she knew that.

She was nearly beside him—it was the most dangerous part. Once they felt she was sufficiently far from the serum bottles not to damage them, they would make their play.

Rourke shouted, "A little change in the plan, Colonel. Anybody blinks an eye and I blow away all the bottles."

"That was not the agreement, Doctor." Rozhdestvenskiy started forward. Rourke pulled the trigger on the rifle—Natalia was clear now, his right hand raising as he blasted three of the serum bottles with the burst.

"A warning," Rourke shouted.

"Don't shoot," Rozhdestvenskiy commanded his men.

Natalia stood beside Rourke now.

"You plan what I think?"

"You plan what I think?" he asked back.

"Yes—I love you, John."

She dropped the bottle at her side to the floor. It shattered, the liquid inside splashing up on Rourke's feet and hers.

"What are you doing?" Rozhdestvenskiy screamed the words.

Rourke never moved the muzzles of his rifles, but Natalia wheeled beside him, her rifles pointed toward the truck. "There are five bottles in the truck, Colonel. John will now destroy the serum in the bottles by the wall. You cannot stop him before he empties both rifles and destroys the bottles utterly. If you attempt to do so, I shall destroy those bottles in the truck."

"You would kill Rourke with the explosives!"

"You would kill him by shooting him—and the rifles were never loaded with explosives—I fooled you, Colonel. The

195

master spy duped — what a tragedy!"

"Bitch — "

"Right now I'm planning to shoot the serum bottles," Rourke snarled. "I can shoot you, too. Look at it this way — as long as we have the five bottles in the truck, you've got a chance." Rourke emptied the assault rifles into the serum bottles at the far side of the laboratory — not a move made to stop him. The bottles seemed to shatter in slow motion, shards of glass everywhere, bottles shattering other bottles, the shelves starting to collapse.

One bottle remained.

Rourke let the emptied M-16s fall to his sides. He drew the Python, saying, "If only a few ccs are needed for each injection, well, we probably have enough in the truck to inject your entire Elite Corps and all of the women — think about that. This is a Colt — Natalia tells me you carry one, too. A Colt is a very American gun — Colt's sort of like apple pie, baseball, motherhood." He thumbcocked the Metalifed and Mag-na-ported six-inch, firing once, the last bottle shattering.

Rourke let himself smile.

"Now, Colonel, Natalia's going to get on the truck in just a minute here, and I'll keep one of my assault rifles trained on the five bottles that are left. She'll drive off and I'll follow her. Then we'll see what happens." Rourke holstered the Python, then dumped the empty magazines from the assault rifles, letting them clatter to the floor. He reloaded. He backstepped through the doorway, Natalia still aimed both rifles at the five bottles in the truck bed.

Rourke turned, running along the loading dock, jumping aboard the fire engine red Ninja bike, swinging both M-16s toward the truck bed. He couldn't miss at the range. He let the rifles fall to his sides, "Not yet, Natalia." He started the bike, turning it around to face the ramp. He leveled one of the M-16s toward the five bottles. "Now — remind our friends."

196

He couldn't see inside, but he heard Natalia calling over her shoulder, "Doctor Rourke has the five remaining bottles under the muzzle of his rifle. I am boarding the truck. At the first shot, the first attempt to stop us of any kind, he shall destroy the remaining five bottles. Maybe you can scrape some off the floor and filter out the broken glass — but I don't think so."

"Damn you!" It was Rozhdestvenskiy's voice. But Natalia only walked ahead, slowly, down the ramp, around the cab of the pickup, setting both rifles inside, climbing in behind the wheel. The engine started. The truck lurched slightly forward. Rourke turned and looked behind him, but the rifle's muzzle unswerving. He shouted, "Natalia, get moving — Rozhdestvenskiy, bite my ass," and Rourke swung the second M-16 toward the laboratory doors, firing half a magazine, the Elite Corps dropping back, Rourke letting both rifles fall to his sides, putting himself low over the Ninja's body, letting the bike out and taking it down the ramp — he was trying to match the zero to sixty figures he'd read of.

Chapter Sixty-four

Rozhdestvenskiy jumped from the loading dock, tossing his car keys in his hand. "What about the force that fought at the small corridor?"

"They were Russians, Comrade Colonel," the lieutenant answered. "They were Special Forces—the unit known as Fight—they—"

"Are they dead—I did not ask for them to be eulogized."

"They are dead—but so few of them, Comrade Colonel—they killed sixty-three of our men."

Rozhdestvenskiy looked at the young lieutenant. "And what of the particle beam facility?"

"The Americans have all been killed. But the doors leading into the facility were mined, and have only just been gotten through."

"Idiots, so some of the Americans are inside."

"Only one it is thought, Comrade Colonel—but Comrade Colonel—"

"What?"

"In the battle between our men and the Special Forces unit, Major Revnik was killed by the Special Forces Captain."

"Then Revnik is dead—if he were stupid enough to die, he was too stupid to live." He gestured after Rourke and Natalia Tiemerovna. "Seal off all passages. The women can fight as well. Leave a wide path for them. They must be heading for the doors to the airfield elevators. We shall pursue them, overtake them and kill Rourke before he can destroy the serum bottles. Then our assault vans can box in Major Tiemerovna's truck and she can be killed. We shall still be triumphant. But there is to be no shooting at the truck itself. No one but this unit is to attack them. The function of the rest of my forces is merely to contain them — no risks can be taken with the bottles. I want one hundred men — or men and women — it doesn't matter — I want them on the field in the event Rourke and the major slip through our fingers. If the airplane should reach the field before interception, it should be destroyed."

"But the serum, Comrade Colonel — "

"Better no one should survive than Rourke and Major Tiemerovna, Lieutenant. We can easily catch them. The motorcycle is capable of great speed, but the truck is not. In the corridor straightaways, we can catch them. And we can kill them."

He started to walk across the boxlike chamber. Near the far corridor, in a storage compartment, the vehicles were garaged.

He checked the revolver in his belt. He would get Rourke and Natalia Tiemerovna — it was more important now than life itself.

Rozhdestvenskiy started to run.

Chapter Sixty-five

The truck, with its heavy load, would barely do sixty steadily, Rourke judged, comparing the truck's speed with the matching speed of the Ninja, and only on the straightaways. It was necessary in the curves, to preserve the load, to slow to thirty.

Behind him he heard what he had expected to hear—vehicles.

Rourke looked back. Coming around the curve behind them, into the straightaway were what he counted as an even dozen more or less Honda Gold Wings, fast, powerful, painted black. Behind the wedge of bikers a single automobile—a black Pontiac Firebird Trans-Am. Behind this, two abreast, black painted vans. Visible on the roofs of the vans some type of weapon—he imagined Soviet RPK light machineguns.

"Natalia! Company. Hustle," he shouted.

He saw her through the open window, turning her head, glance at him once—her eyes in the pale green of the overhead lighting system—their blueness riveted him.

The truck began to pick up speed, but it couldn't pick up much with the specialized emission control equipment it carried, and acceleration was pitifully slow.

He looked behind him again—the KGB armada was closing.

They would target him, so he couldn't destroy the serum in the truck bed. Then close in on Natalia and box the pickup in, killing her and rescuing the serum. It was Rozhdestvenskiy's only option.

The thought flashed across Rourke's mind, to abandon

the motorcycle and jump into the pickup bed, but it wouldn't prevent them from stopping the truck. He could destroy the serum, but he needed the serum to keep his wife, his children, Paul alive.

And Rozhdestvenskiy would know Rourke wanted at least some of the serum intact.

"May as well get started," he whispered into the slipstream around him. He stabbed the left side M-16 toward the KGB armada and opened fire, emptying the half spent magazine, one of the bikes swerving, spinning out, crashing against the concrete surface of the walkway on the left side of the corridor.

Rourke let the rifle fall empty to his side, making the bike accelerate, outstripping Natalia and the truck for an instant, the road surface around him that formed the corridor floor taking the impact of bursts of machinegun fire, slugs whistling, ricocheting maddeningly.

Rourke pulled in front of the truck, using the serum bottles it contained as a shield, the gunfire ceasing, but as he looked back, the motorcycles and the Firebird speeding ahead.

Rourke let the Ninja drift right, bringing up the second M-16, firing behind him—spraying the assault rifle left to right and back again, three of the bikers down, their machines spinning out, crashing against the walkway bases, others of the machines slowing, skidding, another bike out of control, crashing.

Rourke let the Ninja drift left as machinegun fire raked the road surface, but it meticulously avoided Natalia in the truck.

Mentally he ran the scorecard—seven bikers remaining, the four vans and the Firebird.

"Shit," he snarled into the wind.

Chapter Sixty-six

Natalia was honking at him, Rourke looking back — she was waving her right hand. Rourke shook his head, not understanding.

Natalia began to honk her horn again — long and short blasts of the horn — suddenly Rourke realized. Morse code. Rourke turned to her again moving his right hand as if in a wiping out motion, then nodding his head.

She nodded back.

Dash — dot — dash — dot.

Dot — dot — dash — dot. Dash — dash — dash. Dot — dot — dash. Dot — dash — dot.

"C-4," Rourke whispered. "C-4."

He turned to her, nodding. The musette bag on his left side — the five pounds of C-4 he himself had taken. He reached into the musette bag, awkwardly one handed clawing at the brick of plastique, ripping away approximately a third of it. He kneaded it in his hand, like some persons use a rubber ball to exercise their fingers. It was becoming soft from his body heat.

Rourke kept kneading it, already knowing what he would do with it.

Rourke let the Ninja drift right, the ball of C-4 in his right hand — he snapped his right arm back and outward, the C-4 leaving his grip, edging slightly left in the bike's saddle, keeping his balance, drawing the Python.

The seven bikers were coming — he let them come, past the C-4 almost. He stabbed the Python behind him, gunfire from the vans hammering into the pavement around him. He double actioned the Python once. A miss. Again. Another miss.

The bikers were nearly past it. He fired the Python once more—there was a roar, screams drowned in it, Rourke nearly losing the bike, swinging his balance right again, looking back, a fireball belched upward toward the corridor ceiling, chunks of human beings and motorcycles rained downward.

The Trans-Am had swerved, taken one of the small ramps leading to the walkway, moving along the walkway, now, coming fast, bouncing between the wall to the right and the walkway guard rail to the left, sparks flying as the fenders grated against the railing, the driver's side window rolling down, the muzzle of a submachinegun poking through it. And his lips drawn back against the slipstream of the wind, Rozhdestvenskiy screaming the word, "Die!"

Rourke made the bike swerve, the chattering sound of glass—he looked to his left—Rozhdestvenskiy was shooting at Natalia, the windshield cracked, the pickup swerving, then steadying.

The Python still in his right fist, Rourke stabbed it toward the black sportscar, firing twice for the window, missing, seeing the sparks as the bullets glanced off the hood.

The subgun opened up again, Rourke ramming the Python into the leather, making the bike speed ahead.

He glanced behind him—one of the vans had somehow become disabled. Only three remained, machinegun fire coming toward him now as all three formed a single rank across the corridor floor.

Subgun fire from the Pontiac to his right. The Firebird was speeding up, past Natalia, even with Rourke.

Rourke swung the M-16 outward, pumping the trigger, emptying the magazine toward the Firebird, the Firebird veered left—the railing on the walkway peeled away, chunks of it flying outward into the corridor road surface, Rourke dropping the empty M-16 from his fist, making the Ninja swerve away.

He looked back and right—the Firebird was still coming, and behind him now, the three vans had stopped shooting; they were closing with Natalia.

More subgun fire from the Firebird, Rourke reaching to the small of his back to the Thad Rybka holster and the two-inch Colt Lawman. He had it, pointing the little .357 toward the Firebird, firing, but not for the passenger compartment and the open window there—for the tires instead. At the speeds with which the car moved, the tires were high speed radials, not run-flats. He aimed for the area by the rims, the left front so he would affect the steering. He doubled actioned the little Colt. A miss.

Subgun fire from the window again. Rourke fired the little Colt—once, twice, a third time—four rounds were gone.

Subgun fire—he could smell gasoline—the submachine-gun Rozhdestvenskiy used had hit the Ninja's gas tank. It could explode at any moment.

Rourke pumped the last two rounds from the Lawman—the tire seemed to explode, the Firebird crashing through the guard rail, bouncing back against the concrete to the right of the car, then away, punching out the railing, crashing down to the road surface, rolling, sliding along on the roof. Rourke swerved the Ninja, the little Colt shoved into his belt.

He let the bike skid, away from him, jumping clear, the bike skidding now toward the Firebird, the bike impacting against the passenger door of the inverted street machine—the gasoline tank—a small explosion, flames scorching upward for a brief instant, the Firebird's tires on fire.

Rourke rolled across the road surface, stopping on his back, remembering to breathe.

He was up—no time to finish Rozhdestvenskiy if he weren't already dead—the vans were coming, closing in on Natalia. Rourke reached for the C-4 in his musette bag—about three pounds of it, molding it quickly into a ball, the

C-4 already slightly warm from his body heat.

He threw the C-4 into the roadway, one of the vans skidding away, hitting the walkway to Rourke's right, exploding, flames belching upward.

Rourke drew both Detonics pistols simultaneously, firing, aiming for the C-4, machinegun fire from the two remaining vans hammering at him, around him, chips of concrete flying, bullets ricocheting.

The two vans were near the C-4 now, Natalia well past it.

A hit—the C-4 exploded, Natalia's truck swerving, the left fender glancing off the walkway, the truck bouncing, lurching, but moving ahead.

One van gone. The other still coming.

The pickup slowed, Rourke running for it, stabbing both pistols into his belt, jumping, clawing for the side of the truck bed, his fingers closing for it, hurtling his body weight over and inside, rolling, crashing against the coffin-shaped boxes of the cryogenic chambers.

Rourke picked himself up to his knees, changing sticks for the Detonics pistols. As the pickup swerved to avoid the wreckage of the Firebird and the motorcycle, Rourke saw Rozhdestvenskiy, crawling, alive, away from the wreckage, and for a second their eyes met.

The last van was still coming. Rozhdestvenskiy's voice echoed through the corridor. "Kill them!"

Chapter Sixty-seven

Reed climbed, glancing to the Timex on his left wrist, smudging away the blood from the crystal. If what he had done to the particle beam system worked, the system would explode in a matter of minutes, he reasoned.

He was still only a third of the way up the gantry, the American flag beneath his fatigue blouse still, his .45, half-loaded only, in the military flap holster at his belt. The second .45 he had carried for a time he had lost in battle.

He kept climbing, his right palm bloody and raw from scraping against the metal, his left arm blessedly numbed to the pain there, his abdomen hurting — he felt like throwing up but didn't dare. When he coughed, blood spurted out.

He kept moving.

Soon — very soon.

The sun was truly setting and he noticed it more than he had ever before — very red, very beautiful.

He kept climbing.

It was the one thing he had to do.

Chapter Sixty-eight

Rourke climbed around from the truck bed, reaching for the passenger side door, Natalia springing the door as he shouted to her, Rourke swinging his left leg inside, then falling to his knees on the seat.

He twisted around, the M-16s making movement in so confined a space awkward, Natalia saying as he slammed the door closed, "We should be just a few minutes away from the bombproof doors leading into the hangar bays — if the doors are still opened."

"They're gonna want to stop us, not just box us in, Rozhdestvenskiy had to figure on that. Unless he gets on a radio and tells them to close, they should be open — anyway — they can't stop their supply shipments just for us — we gotta worry about that last van."

Exhausted, Rourke unslung the M-16s from his shoulders, leaning through the window. The van was closing, the LMG beginning to open up. Rourke fired the M-16, toward the windshield — but it would be bullet proofed.

The slugs had no effect.

"Give this thing all the gas it's got," he roared to Natalia. "And gimme the extra C-4 you took off the American corporal's body. If those doors to the hangar bays are closed, it won't get us through anyway."

"Agreed." Natalia pushed her black canvas bag across the seat. "It's inside."

Rourke opened the bag — a nightgown, a hair brush, a half-dozen speed-loaders for the L-Frames she carried.

It wasn't in the outside pouch. He zipped open the main compartment — the C-4, beside it tampons and a half-emptied carton of cigarettes. "Women," Rourke murmured. He took the C-4, snapping the brick in half, then began kneading it in his hands, the other half returned to the bag. It was starting to soften.

"I'd say hurry up, he's closing on us." Gunfire hit the wall to their left, a ricochet cracking more of the windshield, Natalia making the truck swerve, then straightening. "The turn-off should be up here."

"Right. You let me off when you take it, then drive like hell for a hundred yards or so. And fast." Rourke formed the C-4 into a mushroom shape — it was the consistency of the Play-Doh his children had used when they were small.

"Here it is," Natalia shouted, the truck skidding, the rear end fishtailing, Natalia downshifting, fighting the wheel, the truck turning, the cargo shifting behind them — Rourke heard the sound of glass breaking.

One of the bottles of serum — had any of it survived?

She turned the truck into the access corridor, Rourke swinging open the door, the truck slowing, Rourke jumping down, falling to his knees, shouting, "Get outta here."

The van was making the turn. Rourke waited, the van coming, the LMG starting to fire again, slugs hammering the concrete wall of the corridor.

Rourke had the reloaded Python in his left fist. In his right the mushroom shaped chunk of plastique, soft at the top, very soft.

He hurled the C-4, shifting the Python to his right fist, the C-4 hitting the grill at the front of the van, molding around the metal, sticking there.

Rourke fired at the van — a miss, the van still coming, Rourke running, running harder than he had ever run in his life.

To his right ahead was a small access tunnel. Rourke jumped to the walkway, vaulting the railing, stabbing the Python outward as a line of machinegun fire etched along the wall surface toward him.

He double actioned the Python once, diving to the small access tunnel, the roar deafening as he covered his ears and hugged his forearms against the sides of his head—he could feel the force of the explosion tearing at him, feel the heat of it.

The explosion died.

Rourke got to his knees—part of his shirt had been torn away.

He stood up, his hands shook.

He stooped over, picking up the Python.

He stepped to the end of the access tunnel. The van was a mass of twisted metal, still smoldering, the upholstery burning in patches along the road surface.

Ahead of him, Natalia had stopped the truck. She was reversing, Rourke started to run to meet her.

If the serum had survived—even a little of it, he could at least save Sarah and the children, Paul and Natalia—at least them.

If the bombproof doors to the hangar bays were only open.

He kept running, the Python still in his right hand.

Chapter Sixty-nine

The bombproof doors had been open—maybe he live, right, he thought. The door on the pickup's passenger sid wide open, Rourke hugged the doorframe, firing out firs one, then the second of his two M-16s, cutting down per haps a dozen of the KGB hangar bay personnel, the res running back through the doors.

Rourke jumped clear as Natalia slowed the pickup.

"I'll find us a plane. You get those doors sealed—th mechanism's over there," and he pointed to the far wall.

He started running across the hangar bay, searching fo the right aircraft, sufficiently large to handle the cargo, suf ficiently fast to get them where they needed to go, with littl enough landing field required to put her down.

That the hangar bay doors had been open told him on thing—Rozhdestvenskiy would be waiting to stop them o the field above.

He found the plane, stopping before it—a substantiall modified Grumman OV-1 Mohawk of the type used in Viet nam. He ran to it, to begin pre-flighting. Already, th bombproof doors were closing behind him . . .

It wasn't the perfect aircraft, it required too much run way space for landing, but he could set it down on a high way and then taxi it off the road. With luck he'd make i close enough to the motorcycle he had left behind, hidde in the trees near the field he had used when he'd landed th prototype jet fighter, the same craft they had used to fly t Chicago to see Varakov.

With the truck back near the cargo doors, and Natalia' help, he had loaded his backpack, the six cryogenics cham ers, the six spare parts kits for the chambers, the six monitoring consoles, the six spare parts kits for the monitoring equipment—and the one remaining jar of the serum—the others destroyed.

Rourke sat at the controls now, the plane ready as it would ever be, Natalia working the elevator controls.

Overhead, the sky was darkening. At any moment, the bombproof shields would slide in place automatically, blocking the elevator shaft.

There had been no sounds of gunfire from the field above, and as the overhead section of the runway slipped further and further apart, there was still no sound.

His only sensation was the purple darkness.

He looked out. Natalia ran to board the aircraft, jumping, the elevator already in motion, Natalia reaching the elevator and running for the aircraft.

She was aboard, Rourke hearing the sounds of the hatch being closed.

"I'm all set," she called out, breathless sounding. Rourke nodded, both M-16s loaded, his pistols checked. Natalia took up her position by the co-pilot's controls, two M-16s beside her. There would be no way to have a protracted gun battle from the aircraft—it would be take-off or lose.

Rourke raced the engines, the plane starting to inch ahead, the elevator nearly to the level of the field.

Already, he could see KGB Elite Corps ringing the opening for the elevator pad, M-16s in their hands. Behind them, Jeeps fitted with RPK light machineguns.

Rozhdestvenskiy's face in the lights of the field as the elevator pad settled.

Rourke hit both engines, starting ahead, Rozhdestvenskiy's voice loud over a bullhorn, "Surrender now and you will have merciful deaths. If you force us to destroy the last of the cryogenic serum, you will take weeks to die in agony, Rourke. Hear me. And you will watch Natalia Tiemerovna die first. I will flay her skin an inch at a time, I

211

will have my men rape her before your eyes. Surrender or face this."

He could run down the men with the airplane, but the bodies were so densely packed together that they would eventually block the aircraft's wheels. The Jeeps formed a solid wall beyond that.

They were trapped.

"Be ready to fight," Rourke whispered. "I can't get us off the ground. And I'll kill you just before it ends — Rozhdest venskiy meant what he said."

Natalia whispered, "Yes."

"Turn one of your M-16s against the bottle of the serum. Do it now." Rourke still had almost full power to the engines, ready for take-off. "Damnit," he swore.

He saw Rozhdestvenskiy's face, the KGB colonel standing in the front passenger side of one of the Jeeps, his left arm casually draped over the RPK — he was smiling.

Perhaps, Rourke thought, before they swarmed over the plane, he could get off a shot to kill Rozhdestvenskiy.

He — Rourke — and Natalia and, the ones who had died had won in a way, Rourke thought. Rozhdestvenskiy and his men were doomed without the serum. Perhaps successive generations of them could breed inside the Womb until it was safe to return to the surface, perhaps somehow they would not be so horribly evil. That the Womb still was capable of hermetic seal was the only defeat. His own death. Natalia's death — considering they had destroyed Rozhdestvenskiy's plans for survival — these mattered little. Paul. Sarah. Michael. Annie. That they would die, that he had failed them consumed him, burning in him, angering him.

"The hell with this. I'll blow up the damned plane all over them — hold on — don't shoot the serum bottle yet," and Rourke throttled forward, the aircraft starting to move.

"Surrender, Rourke!"

Rozhdestvenskiy couldn't hear him, but Rourke shouted

212

it anyway, "Bite my ass, you bastard!"

He gave the plane full throttle, the KGB guards moving back, but the Jeeps unmoving, the machinegunners moving their weapons into position. It was all about to go.

An explosion, louder than anything Rourke had ever heard before. He looked to his left—the top of the mountain—a mushroom shaped ball of fire rising skyward—and in its light on one of the twin gantries there, a figure. Something about it—it had to be Reed. And in the instant of light, draped across Reed's body nearly to the top of the gantry but not quite reaching it, blew an American flag in the heat wind.

Rourke gave the craft more throttle, the Jeeps starting to move now, Rozhdestvenskiy nearly falling from his perch beside one of the RPKs, the vehicle streaking away from the mountain. Already, Rozhdestvenskiy was screaming through the bullhorn, "You will die for this—"

"That's just like a neutron bomb, that's why they're running like hell to get out of here—hang on," and Rourke pushed the throttle all the way forward, working the flaps, steering the craft along the field, threading his way through the maze of running men and fleeing vehicles, the end of the runway nearing as he straightened out. Only one vehicle followed them—the Jeep Rozdestvenskiy had been on, Rozhdestvenskiy driving it now—a pistol in his hand, firing. Rourke gave the aircraft full throttle, the barricade fences coming up fast.

In the sideview mirror of the fuselage, Rozhdestvenskiy, the Jeep skidding, Rozhdestvenskiy's face twisted with rage, his mouth open, screaming words Rourke didn't need to hear to understand.

The barricade fences—full power, the nose coming up. "Hang on," Rourke rasped, Natalia answering nothing, the nose staying up, the barricade fences beneath them now, Rourke hitting the landing gear, hauling it up, banking the aircraft—and as he turned it, the top of the mountain was a ball of flames, the particle beam weapons gone, Reed gone, the flag gone.

On the field beneath them, the Jeeps and figures of running men were like something seen through a microscope.

The neutron radiation would have been minimal and the likelihood of contamination remote. He felt no ill effects, nor apparently did Natalia as he looked at her.

"We made it," she whispered.

"He'll come after us, try to find the Retreat—he'll come."

Rourke said nothing else. It was full night and the world might end before dawn the next day was through.

Chapter Seventy

Colonel Nehemiah Rozhdestvenskiy leaned against one of the Jeeps, staring, staring at his mountain without a top, his mountain that no longer could be hermetically sealed, the Womb that was now useless to him.

One of his officers, Captain Andreki, was calling to him. "Comrade Colonel—the radiation—we must escape before it can reach the airfield—when the cloud settles—"

"I will kill him, then I will die. But I will kill him. It is Doctor Rourke who has done this. And it is Rourke who will die for it. All radar installations which still function are to search for his plane. All ground forces are to search for it above them. We shall take whatever means at our disposal and go to northeastern Georgia. We shall search the mountains there throughout the night. We shall find this Retreat, we shall destroy it, destroy Rourke and Major Tiemerovna, destroy Rourke's family. We shall have the last victory—we shall have the last victory—"

He realized that Captain Andreki was leading him away—but he would pursue Rourke—and inside him he knew this would be the last night of earth.

Chapter Seventy-one

General Ishmael Varakov listened to her words, carefully. "Moscow is gone. The radio was full of static and then for an instant it cleared. All the radio operator could say was 'fire'—and then there was nothing more, not even static, not a sound as though—"

"Enough, Catherine. It has begun. Come stand beside me and we shall talk. You can tell me of your childhood perhaps. We have one night in which to tell each other all that we might ever wish to tell each other," and he smiled at her, taking her hand, slowly walking from his desk toward the figures of the two mastodons at the center of the museum's great hall. His feet hurt. "When I was a boy, all was in turmoil. Russia had suffered defeat at the hands of the Japanese and the old Czar and his family liked more to play tennis and to have parties than to care for the people. Lenin was always on the lips of the people—he is here, he is there. There was much hunger. And then of course the First World War, which was to be the war to end all wars, but so many of our soldiers never returned and then the era of Kerenski, and that failed, and then Lenin finally took charge and there was fighting everywhere. I was only very young after all that and I remember the horrors still as though I had seen them myself because still my family spoke of them, still whispered of them when there was darkness. And the Second World War—in which I fought—Stalin was a fool to ever trust the Nazis. And then they turned on us and tried to destroy us and later we destroyed them. All this—you would think, Catherine, that with all the millions who died in the First War, the many who died during the Revolution, the millions who died during the Second War—you would think that we would have learned something, Catherine, something to tell young people like you that would magically make you understand how stupid and useless it all was. But did we?"

He stopped walking, looking into her eyes. "You are a pretty young girl. I do not still understand why you would so favor an old man by loving him. But I am glad that you do. Sit and tell me about your childhood."

He sat near the feet of the mastodons, Catherine sitting beside, but more perched on the edge of the vinyl covered bench than actually sitting. "I did nothing interesting, Comrade General—it is a very boring story—there is nothing interesting about me—"

"How wrong you are," and he held her hand.

Chapter Seventy-two

He had landed the aircraft on a stretch of straight highway, then taxied it off the road and into a field before it had been able to go no further.

Natalia had gone on ahead, to the original take-off site they had used with the prototype fighter. Rourke's Harley was hidden there.

And Rourke had worked while she had been gone, getting the eighteen smaller crates offloaded from the plane, getting the six coffin-shaped crates which contained the cryogenic chambers nearer to the hatch.

He had field stripped his rifles one at a time, cleaning them. He had cleaned the Government Model, the little Lawman, the six-inch Python. He had touched up the edges of his knives. He had done everything to avoid thinking.

It was already the new day beyond the ocean—and soon—He somehow knew that it was the last day.

A plan had already formed, a plan to solve the unsolveable.

But it meant putting himself in the position of God—and it was an uncomfortable thought.

He loved Sarah. He loved Natalia. He loved them equally—at least he told himself that—and he loved them differently.

It was the only way to solve it.

He closed his eyes. There was no need, no desire to sleep. If all went well and they were able to utilize the cryogenics equipment and the last precious bottle of the serum, he would sleep for nearly five centuries. If it did not, he would die. In either event sleep now was unimportant.

In the distance now, he heard the sound of the trucks, the familiar sound of his own camouflaged Ford pickup truck. The less familiar sounds of the truck he had borrowed from Pete Critchfield, the Resistance leader; Rourke would never return it.

He wondered if Natalia had told Paul and Sarah and the children what would happen at the next dawn. Had she told Paul the story Reed had recounted of the death of Paul's parents?

He somehow doubted that she had. It was, after all, his responsibility.

One could escape one's enemies, but never the ultimate enemy of being the one who was responsible.

He closed his eyes again. There was no need to see the trucks as they approached. And he wondered how he would begin it. Would he look at Michael and Annie and tell them, "Your lives are forever to be changed—forever."

Chapter Seventy-three

He didn't know why the KGB was evacuating the city. There were still regular army troops, but they fought everywhere throughout the city with the people he and the others of the Resistance had freed from the detention camps.

That death was inevitable did not escape him, but not from his wounds at least. He rested in the back of the van they had taken from the Russians, a police van. Through the open doors, he could see Marty approaching, carrying something.

He didn't try to sit up. He watched instead.

Marty stopped at the open rear doors. "Hey, Tommy — how you feeling?"

"I've felt better — what have you got there?"

"Remember I promised you a beer? Well, this one closet near where the locker rooms were — guess one of the KGB prison guards liked beer. Had a cooler-full. I got us each one."

Marty stepped up into the van, twisting the cap off one of the bottles and handing it to Maus. "You heard something, didn't you?"

"Well, you know how people talk — word is the KGB pulled out because some top secret project went belly up — and — " But he stopped talking.

"And what?"

"Nothin' important — "

"What?"

Marty opened his beer, clinked the bottle against Maus's bottle and then took a long pull. He smacked his lips. "Nice and cold."

"What?"

"They had a radio here—one of those jobbies that pulls in stations from all over the place." Marty drank some more of the beer. "Got a ham operator out of Greenland—said all of Europe was off the air—lots of static, then a moment of clear transmission—one of the guys he had talked to—he said the—" Marty took another pull on the beer. "Trouble with beer—once you drink it, the bottle's empty." And he looked at Maus. "The ham operator said the guy told him the sky was on fire and—it didn't make much sense."

Maus raised his bottle of beer, clinked the glass against Marty's. "Here's lookin' at ya, Marty."

Marty began to laugh. "I betchya I can scrounge up a couple more beers if I try hard. Our work's done tonight."

"Yeah, that's a good idea. You know, I had this terrific idea for increasing sales, ya know—was just gonna implement it before The Night of The War."

"What kinda idea?"

"It'll take a while to explain it—"

Marty laughed, and Maus laughed then, too. Marty said, "I got all night, Tommy."

Chapter Seventy-four

President Samuel Chambers stood on the rise of ground looking out. He could see much by the fires that still burned. Beside him stood Lieutenant Feltcher. At the base of the rise stood the TVM Commander.

The Soviet Armies had been defeated, routed.

Feltcher said, "We won, Mr. President."

"My radio man has been getting these weird signals all night. Ham operators—like that."

"What do you mean, sir?"

He looked at Feltcher.

He didn't have the heart to tell him. Instead, he said, "Maybe what transpired will bring about peace someday. Maybe somebody somewhere will look back and know what happened—maybe."

"You mean, Mr. President, maybe we whipped them so bad we'll really beat them, drive 'em back to the Soviet Union—have America back?"

"By tomorrow morning, I'm confident of it, Lieutenant, all our troubles will be over."

"Is it some new weapon, sir?"

He looked at Feltcher in the firelight, then just shook his head as he lit a cigarette—he had several packs to still smoke that night—there was no sense wasting the last of his cigarettes. "No—not a new weapon, Lieutenant. I think we'll shortly see the old weapons did quite enough—quite enough." He inhaled the smoke deep into his lungs and said nothing else for a moment.

Then he looked at Feltcher. "While you were away, well, it's too long a story. But I'll tell you anyway. We did something to the air and the sky is catching on fire and when the sun rises tomorrow morning we'll all be dead. And there's no way to stop it. I've got a lot of smoking to do — if you want to join me, I'll tell you about it. Or maybe you want to find someplace to go and pray. Up to you, Lieutenant."

Feltcher didn't say anything. After a moment there was a solitary pistol shot. Someone in the darkness, Chambers knew, had just taken his own life rather than face the sunrise. Others had already — others would.

Chambers began to walk toward the tent that was his newest headquarters, his last headquarters. He turned around to look at Feltcher. The young lieutenant was making the sign of the cross.

Chapter Seventy-five

Natalia's knowledge of engineering and electronics, Paul's practical knowledge of how things worked gained from his experience with editing technical writing, Sarah's experience with the practical aspects of nursing and with design, Rourke's own experience with building the Retreat from nothing, with the functioning of the human body.

An engineer turned spy, a trade magazine editor, a would-be nurse turned artist and writer, a doctor turned weapons expert and survivalist. The children served as 'gophers' — go for this and go for that.

Paul with Michael's help had prepared the bikes and the trucks for the long term storage. Sarah, with Annie's help, had prepared the foodstuffs, supervised the plants which renewed the oxygen supply inside the Retreat. They would not last the five hundred years, but with the timer-connected growlights and water sprays, they would thrive long enough that when they awakened in five hundred years if they awakened, the oxygen would be clean to breathe if not very fresh.

They had seen to all of the weapons, seen to the generator systems, the backup generators, all these keyed to the hydroelectric power system based on the underground stream and the waterfall. If this failed, the cryogenic chambers would be their coffins and they would never awaken.

The last of the cables were being strung, linking the cryogenic chambers' monitoring systems to the power supply, Annie feeding cable while Natalia connected it.

Rourke stepped to the electronic monitoring console. There had never been a need for the system before. But he had activated it once they had sealed the main entrance of the Retreat. The two escape chambers had also been checked, Rourke doing this himself. The one tunnel leading through to the other side of the mountain was hermetically sealed, as was the main entrance.

He had not yet hermetically sealed the second tunnel which led above.

Rourke studied the console controls, then looked up to the television monitoring screen—closed circuit, via cable, it would function until the end, until the atmosphere caught fire and the camera and cable just simply burned.

It was nearly dawn. He adjusted the instruments. In the distance near the base of the mountain, he could make out large numbers of troops moving with mechanized equipment.

In the air were helicopters of every description.

These were Rozhdestvenskiy's forces, searching for the Retreat to destroy it.

But the sun was almost rising and throughout the hours they had worked until they could take no more of it, Rourke and the others had listened to shortwave broadcasts—the horror, the devastation. It followed the sun. There had been a ham operator in Greenland who had constantly been broadcasting—about the fires which consumed Europe, England—but now his voice too was stilled.

There had been other broadcasts—U.S. II announcing the victory over the Soviet Forces—Natalia had shown no emotion at this.

Victory, Rourke thought. What a strange word.

"John, all set!" Rubenstein sang out.

Rourke looked behind him, losing his train of thought. "Good, Paul, help Natalia with the injections."

"I'm through here, too," Sarah called out. "I can help; I've used hypodermics before."

"Go ahead then." Rourke stared at the monitor. The sky above the Retreat was almost black, lightning bolts streaking across it, ball lightning—pure electricity—shooting in low arcs under the clouds. Rourke played with the controls. He scanned the valley on zoom and more clearly now could see men and equipment moving toward the mountain road.

He exhaled hard, studying the television picture. There were dozens of helicopters in the air moving along above the men—Soviet. Rourke studied the monitor—the electrical storm was heightening.

"John, the injections are ready, all six."

Rourke looked back at Natalia, then at Rubenstein and at Sarah—the children still moved, talked, but it was as if the three other adults and himself had suddenly frozen—still.

"Good," Rourke finally said. "Isn't much time left. From the way that sky looks, the ionization is already starting."

Rourke started across the room, toward the cryogenic chambers, their blue light bathing the room in a haze.

Rourke glanced back toward the television monitor, the blackening sky, the lightning. "I'll check the last escape hatch and seal it before I put myself under—give everybody the injections first," Rourke said softly.

Rourke walked the few paces to the coffee table, earlier moved out of the way of the chambers and monitoring equipment. Beside his glass fronted gun case now. He looked down at the six hypodermic needles on a white towel there. There was a taped name on each. He picked up the needle for Michael.

"Natalia—you checked my figures—you agree on the amount of the injections."

"There were only tables for body weights down to ninety pounds, John, I worked back through the formula in the manuals accompanying the chambers, Michael weighs sixty-two pounds. The injection should be right."

Rourke looked at the injection, then at his son. "Michael, kiss your mother and sister, then come over to me."

Natalia was beside Rourke in an instant, reaching up,

taking the hypodermic from Rourke's fingers. "I'll give your son the injection — if something — it shouldn't be your guilt, John."

Rourke started to say something, but didn't, just nodding. He watched Michael and his mother hug each other, then watched Annie throw her arms around her brother, kissing him.

Michael walked toward him.

Rourke looked down at the boy. "Michael, it should seem like only a little time. I know five hundred years sounds like a long time, but when you're just sleeping —"

"Will I dream a lot, Daddy?"

Rourke dropped to his knees in front of the boy, squeezing Michael tight against him, and as he spoke his voice sounded choked, strained to him. "Son, you'll dream good dreams, I know you will," Rourke whispered.

He could feel the boy's body tense, Rourke's eyes focusing tight on the needle as it entered his son's arm, then on Natalia's eyes.

"I feel — I feel —"

Rourke stood up, sweeping his son into his arms as the boy fell almost instantly asleep.

"That's supposed to —" Natalia began.

Rourke looked at her, murmuring, "I know, it's supposed to happen."

Rourke carried his son to the cryogenic chamber, resting the tiny body inside it. His eyes flicked from the elapsed time readout setting back to his son's face. The breathing was shallow — too shallow? Rourke listened for the heartbeat with a stethoscope from the small shelf at the side of the chamber. "It's slow — very slow —"

Sarah was beside him, holding Rourke's arm.

Annie, her voice odd sounding, asked, "Is Michael all right?"

Rourke looked down at his daughter and swept her into his arms, tears streaming from his eyes as he held her.

"Michael's all right . . ."

Both children rested under the glowing translucent domes now, their faces bathed in the blue light, clouds of gas beginning to swirl around them. Rourke stared at them. Sarah stood on his right, Rourke's arm around her. Natalia stood at his left, her hand in his. Paul flanked Natalia.

Rourke looked away from the faces of his children. For the last two minutes, the horror show had continued—the Soviet soldiers as they marched up the mountainside were dying, struck by lightning, ball lightning consumed some of them—human torches. Only three of the helicopters remained aloft, burning debris dotting the landscape.

"You'd think they'd give up," Rourke murmured.

"Would you?" Natalia asked softly.

Rourke said nothing. After a long moment, then, "Paul—you're—"

"Yeah—I know—I kind of figured—God," and Rubenstein let out a long, deep breath. "Guess I'd better lie down—in my chamber, huh?"

"Relax, Paul," Rourke whispered, taking the needle, starting toward his friend.

Natalia embraced Rubenstein, kissing him on the lips. Rubenstein stepped back, looking somehow embarrassed. "I'm going to feel—funny, I'm—aw, give it to me," and Rubenstein started to sit down on the edge of his chamber.

Rourke extended his hand, the younger man taking it. "Paul, if I'd had a brother, it would have been you."

The younger man smiled. "I love ya, both of you," and he looked at Natalia then back at Rourke. Already he was rolling up his left sleeve.

"Loosen your belt, kick off your shoes—don't want to constrict your blood vessels. Probably should all be naked."

"I don't think it'll make much difference—if we live, we live—you taught me that," Rubenstein smiled.

Rourke clapped the younger man on the shoulder, saying, "Until we wake up then."

Rubenstein's eyes were on the needle. Rourke started to put the needle to Rubenstein's arm. Rubenstein blocked Rourke's hand for a second, saying sheepishly, "I always hated shots—let me look the other way."

Rourke gave him the injection . . .

Rourke, Sarah and Natalia stood beside the glowing blue lights, the three remaining unoccupied chambers. The electrical storm had intensified still more as Rourke studied the monitor for a moment. Natalia, glancing at Sarah, came into Rourke's arms. Rourke held her.

"Don't feel, well, just don't," Sarah whispered, her voice odd. She turned away, walking over to where the children slept, gas filling the chambers now in a swirling cloud.

"What are our chances?" Natalia whispered to Rourke.

"Natural granite will insulate against electrical shock— should keep the air from burning in here. After we're all in the chambers, we won't need air anyway. We'll breathe the gas—it's continuously purified. The plants over there will keep growing," and he gestured beyond the far end of the great room, the plastic covered greenhouse there with the purple grow lights. "The underground springs should keep up our electrical power. Those grow lights should burn for years with the timers before the fluorescent tubes die—the plants will clean the air we breathed now so there'll be clean air inside the Retreat when we awaken. Stale—but it'll be clean. Nothing else on earth—unless it's sealed in granite— nothing should survive, live. We have the only chambers that will work because we have the only serum."

"The Eden Project—"

"If there wasn't a meteor shower that got their hulls, or there wasn't a malfunction in their solar batteries, or something else no one foresaw—they would be back after we awaken."

"I feel," Natalia whispered, "feels like, like the harlot or something—" She glanced at Sarah.

"Don't."

"After we wake up, what—"

"Don't worry—but I know I'm glad you're with me, here."

"Give me the injection, John, unless you want me to administer the injection to—to Sarah, for you."

"You sleep," Rourke whispered to her, bending his face toward hers, kissing her lips.

She closed her eyes and leaned against him, murmuring, "I love you."

"Natalia," Rourke said softly, holding her.

He walked beside her, to her chamber. She sat on the edge of it and their eyes met as Rourke placed the needle against her skin. "I love you," he rasped, giving her the injection. She closed her eyes—he missed the blueness there already. . .

It seemed to Rourke like an eternity, but it had been only minutes by the digital clock on the console beside the television monitor, only minutes since Natalia had given Michael the first injection. Sarah stood beside him. "Thank you for finding us—I think." She smiled oddly. "We'll have lot to talk about—the children, other things. You'd better hurry now."

"You always talked us to death," Rourke whispered, chilling at the word. He drew his wife into his arms, looked into her face, then kissed her.

"What are you going to do—about us?" she whispered back, kissing him again.

Rourke breathed hard. "Trust me once more?"

"I love you, John Rourke, and I know you love me. Whatever we make of our lives if we wake up, I guess it doesn't matter as much as our loving one another. We should never have married—we both know that. But I love you."

Rourke held her close, walked with her to her chamber.

"Will you be all right—can you get your chamber started after you—"

"I'll give myself the injection just after I start my chamber," he assured her. "I can hold my breath against the gas—I'll be fine."

"I know that," she smiled, leaning up to him, kissing him, holding his hand. "I'll see you in five hundred years." She closed her eyes and sat on the edge of her chamber as Rourke put the needle to her skin.

"I love you," he whispered, and as she sank back, asleep, he said the word, "Sarah."

Chapter Seventy-six

Rourke studied the television monitor. Perhaps a hundred of the KGB troopers remained now, huddled on the ground, lightning smashing into the rocks beside which they took shelter. "Armageddon," he whispered. Two of the helicopters remained airborne, the sky around them alive with electricity. "Rozhdestvenskiy," he said, staring at the monitor as one of the helicopters flew near the camera.

The sky was black, electricity filling the air, arcing across the ground now. He thought of Reed and what he had died doing.

Rourke, the double Alessi rig still across his shoulders, ran the length of the darkened Great Room, the bluish glow of the chambers chilling, eerie somehow. He studied the faces in the chambers, one-by-one, the eyelids closed, the swirling gases marking the faces then seeming to whisk aside. "I have to," he said to them. "I have to do this—show the KGB why they lost, why they'd lose again or anyone else would lose if it happened all over again."

Rourke started to run again, past the far side of the Great Room, into the storage area.

In the dim light, he ran along the room's length, past the rows of shelves and the provisions there, the ammunition, the spare parts, the clothes—stopping by a small niche in the wall, a steel tool cabinet there. He threw his body against the tool cabinet, budging it aside, then shifting it away from the wall with his hands. There was a steel door, three feet square, a combination lock on it. He twirled the dial on the lock, right, then left, then right, twisting the handle, the door swinging out.

Rourke walked back to the shelves, pulling down a flashlight. He smiled—it was one of the angleheads he and Rubenstein had taken from the geological supply shop in Albuquerque—when it had all begun. He flicked the switch, nothing. He unscrewed the butt cap, reaching into another shelf, and pulling out two batteries, dropping the D-cells into the flashlight and screwing the butt cap closed. He turned toward the small, open steel door, walking toward it. Rourke bent down, flicking on the flashlight, shining it up inside. Rungs were anchored to the living granite, three feet apart, the tunnel inside angling steeply upward.

He turned back to the shelves. From a box he took an American flag. He returned to the escape tunnel.

Rourke pulled himself inside and started to crawl toward the first rung, the flashlight in his left hand. His feet inside, he shone the light toward the door and closed it behind him—there was an identical combination lock on the inside. He wrenched the handle shut, twirling the lock. It was sealed.

Clipping the anglehead flashlight to the front of his shirt, he started to climb, one rung at a time, upward through the darkness. He stopped, before the second door, identical to the first. But only a simple steel bar was across it and he opened it, rubber gaskets on the door itself and on the frame. Rourke crawled through. His feet past the door, he twisted in the narrow tunnel confines, wrenching the door closed behind him, the gaskets sealing.

He kept climbing through the darkness.

The light bouncing, jarring as he moved, he unclipped it from the front of his shirt and shone it ahead. The third sealed doorway. Here too, a simple steel bar locked the door. Rourke started to reach for it, then shone the light to his belt, ripping one of the two snap-held double mag-

233

azine pouches open, off his belt. He slipped the magazines from inside the pouch, opening the pouch's belt slot. With the leather magazine pouch over his left hand like a glove. Rourke reached up for the door handle, twisting away the bar, then wrenching open the handle. The door slid to his right. Above him, the sky rumbled with thunderclaps, massive, unimaginably huge lightning bolts cutting through the clouds, ball lightning rolling from horizon to horizon as he shouldered himself out of the escape tunnel.

Rourke crouched beside the opening at the top of the mountain, electricity arcing through the scrub brush. In the distance, he could see one of the Soviet helicopters crashing down, struck by the lightning, burning. Only one remained. Rourke started to his feet, running, crouched, toward the center of the mountaintop. His radio aerial, camouflaged in a bracken of scrub pine.

Small patches of cloth were visible protruding partially from the inside of his shirt—red and white—as he touched at the flag.

Rourke reached for the antenna mast, electricity sparking from it, Rourke drawing back his hand.

Below him, far beneath the mountain, massive ball lightning rolled across the ground, the ground itself burning, the remaining Russian soldiers running, clothes burning, electricity arcing from their bodies, their heads, bodies exploding with it.

Rourke reached for the mast again, the leather magazine pouch protecting his hand. He started to tug at the cloth, pulling it from inside his shirt. Red. White. Red and white stripes. A blue field with white stars. A strong wind whipped across the mountaintop as Rourke secured the grommets on the flag to the antenna mast, the flag catching in the stiff wind, unfurling, blowing across the top of the mountain.

Rourke stepped back, staring out across the valley. The

thunder seemed to be in waves, lightning bolts ripping the sky around him.

Out of the black sky, the last Soviet helicopter came. Rourke started toward the escape tunnel entrance. The helicopter was firing its machineguns, the rocks around Rourke's feet chipping up, seeming to explode.

A missile launched from the gunship, a smoking trail. It exploded less than a dozen yards from the blowing flag. Rourke fell to the ground, the concussion stunning him. He started to push up to his feet. The flag was ripped, tattered—but still there. The Soviet helicopter was making a run, coming low, its coaxially mounted machineguns blazing, slugs impacting around the flag.

"No-o-o!" Rourke screamed the word, his hands flashing up to the twin stainless Detonics .45s, ripping them from the leather. On the horizon, the sky was burning, like a wave, the fire licking across the air, toward him, engulfing the ground.

Rourke could see inside the cockpit of the helicopter now, past the open cockpit door. "Rozhdestvenskiy," Rourke snarled. The rock floor beneath Rourke chewed up under the impact of the machinegun slugs, a small wound opening on Rourke's left forearm as a rock chip impacted against it. Rourke stood unflinching, the pistols in his hands as the helicopter closed.

Rozhdestvenskiy was leaning out the cockpit door, a submachinegun in his hands, firing.

Rourke shoved both gleaming Detonics .45s ahead of him at arm's length, then started to fire, first the right pistol, then the left, then the right, then the left.

The helicopter was still coming. The slide locked back on the pistol in Rourke's right hand—empty.

Rourke, his lips drawn back over his teeth, shouted, "God Bless America!" The pistol in his left hand discharged, Rozhdestvenskiy's body lurching, twisting, the submachinegun in the KGB colonel's hands firing still, but into the helicopter.

The fire in the sky was rumbling toward Rourke as he started running toward the open hatch of the escape tunnel. He dove for the tunnel; the fire welled up and consumed the mountain, as it had the sky and the earth below . . .

Chapter Seventy-seven

He stood behind the figures of the mastodons, his left arm folded around the shoulders of Catherine — her body trembled.

General Ishmael Varakov waited.

He thought of his niece Natalia.

He thought of the girl beside him who loved him.

He thought of God if there was God and he hoped there was.

He could hear it. The thunder. Outside he could see the lightning in the storm blackened sky.

He had thought to await it staring out across the lake — destruction and beauty co-mingled.

But the museum was his home.

Varakov smiled at the thought.

He had found love in many places. He had found honor. He had found what he felt was truth.

General Varakov held Catherine more closely to him.

He saw it — the wave of fire as it belched through the open brass doors of the museum, washed over and through the mastodons — he did not scream as the fire engulfed him.

MORE EXCITING READING
by William W. Johnstone

OUT OF THE ASHES   (1137, $3.50)

FIRE IN THE ASHES   (1310, $3.50)

ANARCHY IN THE ASHES   (1387, $3.50)

Available wherever paperbacks are sold, or order direct from the Publisher. Send cover price plus 50¢ per copy for mailing and handling to Zebra Books, 475 Park Avenue South, New York, N.Y. 10016. DO NOT SEND CASH.